To my Parents
and in memory of
my Edinburgh upbringing

SCOTTISH
GHOST
STORIES

SCOTTISH GHOST STORIES

EDITED BY GILES GORDON

LOMOND
BOOKS

Scottish Ghost Stories

First published in hardback in Great Britain as *Prevailing Spirits*
by Hamish Hamilton Ltd, 1976. First published in paperback as
Prevailing Spirits by Granada Publishing Ltd in
Panther Books, 1977.

This edition published in 1996 by Senate, an imprint of Random
House UK Ltd, Random House, 20 Vauxhall Bridge Road,
London SW1V 25A.

ISBN 1 85958 483 7

Printed and bound in Guernsey by The Guernsey Press Co. Ltd

Contents

HOLIDAY

The Clark parents had been fighting all day and the child Sheila in the back of the car had been smacked on the knees for nothing but being bored. Now she complained of feeling sick.

'We must stop somewhere here,' said David with determination. Clare was being impossible, talking about hotels and dinner. He pulled up at the side of the one-track road, weary and heavy with sadness. The loch lay before them, not sparkling but shining with a sustained dazzle like the reflection from a mirror. Beyond, it connected with the sea.

Beside the car the perpetual wind buffeted the rushes so that they scraped the bodywork with small creakings. Beyond them a forest of lush bracken rippled and swayed. Beyond the bracken was a band of heather and bog-myrtle leading to the water's edge. The water seemed to have been trimmed neatly round with a rim of short, fine turf from which sprouted clumps of sea-pinks, bleached white. To their left he saw what looked like a track into the bracken and a flat levelled table of grass adjoining a clump of trees. Half of these were dead and covered with lichen, but the others were in leaf and would give shelter.

'There's a spot,' he said, pointing. Clare peered bad-naturedly in the direction indicated. He saw she was not really looking but had withdrawn into her own grievances.

'I can't see anything special about it,' she said.

'I can!' Sheila yelled. She was seven, and never spoke when she could yell. 'It's a super spot. Where all that short grass is, and we can get the caravan down, almost to the water's edge. Let's go there, Mummy, and I can camp like Red Indians! Please!'

'And we're only about a mile from a village,' David added, 'we can go there to shop. This place is called . . .'

– he pulled out the Ordnance map and peered at the section –
'Sgeir an t'Uruisg. Here we are. This rocky bit sticking out.'

Sheila burst out of the car and rushed down the track on
to the plateau. It drummed under the hard heels of her new
brown holiday sandals as she jumped up and down with the
joy of release.

'It's hollow, Daddy!' she yelled.

David joined her.

'It always sounds like that when it's dry.' Clare, beside
them, was regarding the turf with distaste.

'The first thing we'll have to do is sweep off all the sheep
shit. What with that and the rabbits, the place is rather
nasty.'

'It's all dry.'

'Marvellous. What do you want me to do? Make it into
cakes for fuel and light a fire as in Afghanistan? Or should
we smoke it? I don't know where they do that, but I daresay
they do it somewhere!'

He knew it was a nervous habit heightened by their
strained relations, but he felt bitter that she could care so
little about Sheila's enjoyment. It might be their last holiday
all together. He backed the caravan into position, secured it,
and began to unpack, first setting up the tent alongside.
Sheila had collected a sizeable heap of wood and was skip-
ping about the rocky shore, throwing stones. A cloud passed
over the sun, hurling a grey cloak across the scene. The
change was dramatic and frightening. The water, which had
been bright and inviting, turned sullen. The purple heather
became gnarled black witch-roots. Then the cloud rushed
away on its business and the loch beamed. It was as though
a stage manager had been trying his effects. David saw Clare
shiver.

Sheila came pounding back from the small wood, her feet
ringing like horses' hoofs.

'Mummy, Daddy! There's an old ruin in the trees and I've
gathered wood so's we can have a fire!'

'What sort of ruin?' David only half-believed her.

'A house or a barn or something. It still has a fireplace

and most of the chimney and if you look up it there's still soot on it. It could have been a castle!'

'It will be an old farm,' said Clare firmly.

'But it *could* have been a castle,' Sheila maintained tenaciously. Oh God, David thought, just say yes, Clare, just for once.

'It would have to be a lot bigger than that. You know that.'

'Anyway, it's only a heap of stones now and two walls.' Sheila was disappointed again and David was angry at the reason of it. The child was always being emotionally dismembered.

'How are we to get to the village?' demanded Clare from the door of the caravan. She was boiling a kettle and had the irritating habit of turning it every half-minute as though to help it boil. 'Shouldn't we have gone there first? We can't leave the tent and things. Someone could just walk off with them while we're gone.'

Of course she was right. He was such a novice that he had never thought of that. They had borrowed the caravan from the Macadams who had tried to explain everything to them, but this was plain common-sense.

'Nobody would do that. Not in the Highlands.'

'So you say. But only because of the total absence of human life!'

'I'll unhitch. You can be there in ten minutes.' He made it sound simple and hoped to get away with it.

'Oh no, David Clark. I'm not entering a small Scottish village on my own. They don't like English round here.'

'Nonsense.'

'It is not. Look at that old man yesterday when I asked the way. He kept shouting "Eh?" at me in a very strange fashion, then just shrugged and walked off.'

'He was old and deaf. He didn't understand you.'

'So how do I know this village isn't full of old, deaf Scotsmen, who don't understand English?'

'For God's sake, I'll go.'

'And leave me here? This place is frightening. It's black when the sun goes in – you saw it. For "majestic" read "frightening".' David looked at the slopes of black scree. It would get dark quickly when the sun sank. He had never supposed that Clare suffered from claustrophobia. There is menace in a Highland glen.

'Do you realize,' he said, 'that being left here you are statistically about ten thousand times safer than being left in your sitting-room at home. There's practically no crime.'

'There's practically no people! With my luck the first passer-by will be an escaped psychotic from Glasgow.' She rotated the kettle again. It actually began to boil. 'All right,' she said, 'you go. I'll stay in the caravan and lock the door. Leave Sheila with me.'

'She'll want to buy postcards and sweeties.'

'Well she can't. Bring her some and she can wait until tomorrow.'

David crept into the car and drove off feeling ashamed. He saw Sheila running back to the caravan in his rear-view mirror. Her mouth was open and she was shouting for him to stop. Her face was alarmed. Did she think he was leaving? When he was on the road, he wound down the window to yell to her in a cowardly fashion.

'I'm just going to the shops! Back in a minute. I'll bring you something!' She was intercepted by Clare and he revved up and drove on. Sheila was crying and shouting.

He drove up above the loch, zig-zagging on to a low hill where he could see the long narrow expanse of it, stretching like a reptilian tongue to the sea. The day had settled, as so many Highland days do, into late low sunshine. Everything that had been silver was suddenly liquid gold. Here the heather formed a scented crust on the earth and isolated clumps looked like cakes of flowers. Rounding a bend he braked hard, coming upon some advancing sheep. Even they seemed beautified, each wearing a golden fleece. He stopped, when he saw they were the front runners of a flock. A man and two dogs were in attendance at the rear. With the engine stopped and the window open, there was a sublime silence. The wind sighed and high larks were singing. Bees droned in the heather as though they had strict orders to burn up fuel. The sheep passed by, occasionally brushing the wing of the car with their coarse wool. Their feet clattered on the road.

The man was dressed in a rough old pair of trousers, patched jacket and collarless shirt. He carried the usual short crook, an ash-stick with a hand-carved head of ram's horn. On his head he had a flat bonnet that served to mask his face until he was close. His skin was very brown with the weather. Blue eyes looked inquisitively at David from a face that he was surprised to see was that of a young man. The man nodded.

'Grand day.' The remark was not so much a statement on the condition of the weather, as an assertion of his right to occupy the road at his own leisure, when foreigners were abroad.

'It certainly is.'

The courtesy challenge accepted, the man settled comfortably on his crook by David's window, so that his chin rested on the horn head. He was completely at ease, waiting for the sheep to pass. It indicated he was available for talk.

'I'm on my way to Largiemore,' said David. 'Is there a shop there?' It seemed only polite to ask, although he knew the answer.

'There is. There is several in fact.' The man had the soft syllables of a Gaelic speaker. 'It is a long time since I was in Largiemore.' He made it seem like years. 'You are on holiday.' It was a statement.

'Yes. We've just camped down by the loch.'

A sudden change came over the leisurely man. The blue eyes were alarmed.

'Down by the water?' The man lifted his head from the crook and stood by the car window. 'You shouldna' be down by the water. Whereabouts are you?'

'Sgeir an t'Uruisg.'

'You must get out of there!' the man shouted. David wondered if he was entirely sane.

'Why? Will the owner object. It's a nice dry spot. We've been driving all day.'

'There is no owner. Listen to me. You must leave that place. It is no good. Things happen there.' The man was ashen white despite the colour of his skin. David was alarmed.

'Things?'

'I cannot tell you what no man would believe. No mortal thing will go there.'

'There's been sheep. And rabbits.'

'Aye, but not at night. Dinna' delay, move. Round Rhubha Leac to Port an Eas. You'll be safe there.' David was stupefied. He was not sure whether to laugh at this scene from *Macbeth*, or to be alarmed.

'What's there that would harm anyone?'

'No mortal thing but things that have no being on this earth!'

Was this the man's idea of a joke? He looked deadly earnest. The blue eyes were fixed on David's own.

'Where are you bound then?' The man stepped away from the window.

'I'm bound down that way, for my terrible sins. Aye, each night . . .' David did not like the sound of this. He forbore to ask about the 'terrible sins'.

'Thank you for your advice,' he said. 'Where's this I should go?'

'Round Rhubha Leac to Port an Eas. You'll be safe there.'

'Thank you,' David said, starting the engine as the last sheep meandered past. 'Thank you very much.' He started to move the car gently forwards. The man called after him.

'Have you a bairn with you?'

'Yes.'

'Then for the love of God, man, hurry!' David gave him what he hoped was a reassuring wave and drove on, far too fast, to Largiemore. He would ask about the man there. If there was one man in the Highlands not right in the head, he would be sure to bump into Clare.

The village consisted of an outlying crop of pebble-dash

bungalows, and one huddle of white-washed stone houses, separated from the road by a strip of fine grass, well nipped by sheep. He pulled up outside the Post Office and General Stores, and went in hastily. The wobble-on-the-wall bell jangled noisily, but the three women at the counter hardly gave him a glance, except a courtesy 'good day'. They were far too busy confusing their shopping lists and comparing notes about someone called Mary Dewar who ran the Women's Institute. It was dark inside, and crammed to the roof with every sort of unlikely provision. It smelled deliciously of baps, new bread and smoky bacon. A small section was caged off behind light mesh and labelled Post Office. The postmistress woman behind the counter who was about fifty and grey-haired with glasses beckoned him forward with the intention of getting rid of him so that they could continue with their chat. David was embarrassed because of the questions he wanted to ask. The two other ladies, who looked so much like the first they might all have been sisters, stood invitingly back and gave him a sympathetic smile. Just a poor man not knowing what he's doing, they seemed to say. They started up a wholly spurious conversation by the racks of biscuits, where they could listen to every word. He ordered his list of shopping. This was ordinary enough, except for the rather prim way he was handed his cans of beer. In the lull while she rang it all up on the cash register, she slipped in the important question.

'Are you stopping nearby?'

'Yes, camping.'

'Uh-huh.' This was obviously considered an inadequate answer, so he must go on.

'Tell me, I passed a farmer on the road above Sgeir an t'Uruisg. I wondered if I should ask permission to camp?' There was a long, hair-prickling silence. David became aware of a clock on the wall, tocking away the leisurely hours.

'There is no farmer at the Sgeir.'

All the ladies were now staring at him. They were uneasy. Had this been Catholic country he had the feeling they would have crossed themselves.

'There's a ruined clachan down there. And there's been sheep. Someone must own it.'

'The clachan has been deserted these fifty years. It's grazed by Mr Macpherson who lives about ten miles the other side. No one owns it.'

'Someone must.'

'Technically maybe. You're not camped there?'

'Yes!'

There was a concerted intake of breath. David was getting annoyed.

'What's the matter with the place? The man said it was no good.'

'He should know, poor devil, if anyone should.'

'Who is he then?' This was too direct and produced only silence. 'What's not safe about it?'

The customer ladies exchanged glances at the post-mistress lady, who took her cue as their spokeswoman.

'Well, it's a spot that does not get the sun much. It is often in the shade.' She said it with a total lack of conviction. 'The clachan down there does not have much happiness attached.'

The ladies all nodded their heads, spectacles glittering.

'When there is little happiness attached to a place, we always say that the sun goes by it but the clouds are over-head.'

'There was plenty of sun today.'

'Not just the actual sun you understand. It's the feel of a place. Then of course there's the seals.'

'The seals?' He was astonished.

'It's a place they come up, like grey corpses and lie and cry. Almost just like a bairn, is it not, Jessie? It makes the wee short hairs prickle, just at back of your neck.'

Jessie, in a blue twin-set, nodded wisely.

'Aye and we're all good Christians too!'

He drove back fast, concentrating on keeping the car on the road. In a few minutes he was overlooking the loch. There was no sign of the man or the sheep, and the place was still bathed in sunlight. It was strange there was no trace of him.

In a panic he skidded on to the short length of track and jolted up to the caravan, the exhaust whipping and rattling. To his relief, Clare appeared at the door. His heart was thumping as he turned off the engine. He took his time getting out, fiddling with the groceries until he recovered.

'You arrived in a hurry,' Clare remarked.

'Did I?'

'I heard you. You'll wreck the suspension. Did you get the things?'

'Yes, it was even licensed. Where's Sheila?'

'Out there. Is something wrong?' Where Clare had pointed, a large black rock was emerging as the tide ebbed. It was rounded and worn into animal curves so that it appeared to be something stranded. On the end of it, with her feet almost in the water, sat Sheila, staring motionless into the water. Then he saw the seal.

It floated like a blackened skull, nape above water.

'You take the things,' he said to Clare and ran over the turf to the rock. Sheila gave no sign of hearing him approach.

'What are you doing, Sheila?' His voice was breathless and alarmed. The face she turned to him was full of joy.

'I found a seal, Daddy, you can see it. There.'

'I see it.'

'We've been talking to each other.'

David stared at the seal, and the seal seemed to stare back at him. It appeared to have no eyes, but two jelly-filled sockets, slimy as sea-anemones. It lay still as a dead log in the water. A floating skull.

'I've been to the shop,' said David seductively.

'I heard you come back.'

'Don't you want to see what I've got?'

'No. I want to sit with my seal.' David tried to find some reasonable cause for alarm. He could hardly insist she was not to watch seals. He had spent the last three years of her life trying to interest her in birds and animals.

'Your tea will be ready soon.'

'Oh good. Give me a shout. Then I can come back, can't I?'

'You'll have to ask your mother.'

'Oh good!'

David trudged back to the caravan, uneasy. Firstly because of the seal, and secondly because, with the transparent honesty of her age, Sheila knew that Clare only wanted her out of the way.

When she finally left the rock for her tea, there were three seals.

After tea, Sheila got permission from Clare to run off again. David had not told Clare about the shepherd. She would probably make him pack and flee instantly.

'Where are you going,' she demanded, 'aren't you going to dry up?'

David promised, saying he was only going for a stroll and a smoke. He worked his way round so that he could approach unseen through the ruins of the clachan. From these he looked directly on to the whale-backed rock. He could see his daughter sitting by the dark water and was horrified to see that she was throwing sardines to them from a tin that she had evidently stolen. The sardines disintegrated when they hit the water and were ignored. There were now twelve seals and they seemed closer in than before. David flung away his cigarette and clattered over the rock to join her. She had heard him, for the tin was gone.

'What are you doing?' His voice was harsh and panicky.

'Isn't it exciting, Daddy. I just sit and wait and more of them appear. I say "Hello! Please bring your friends!" and they do. I think there are fourteen now.'

'What are they doing?' His voice was too high, and breathless.

'I told you, Daddy, we're talking. I ask them about their life and they ask about mine.'

'You must stop all this nonsense, Sheila. It's getting late and you'll be giving yourself dreams.'

'I won't. They have a beautiful life.'

'I'm not going to argue. It's time you came away from here and got yourself to bed.'

'All right,' she said with amazing docility, 'but we can stay here for a day or two, can't we?'

'We'll see.'

'Good night, seals!' Sheila called, her thin voice soon lost across the black water. The seals remained, staring.

'I'm going to be a Red Indian tonight, aren't I, Daddy!' declared Sheila, trotting across the grass-and-sea-pink verge, holding his hand comfortably tight. 'You did say I could. Please?'

'All right, young lady. The tent is right against the caravan. If you feel cold or lonely or frightened, you're to come inside right away, understand?'

'I understand. But why should I feel lonely or frightened?'

'You just might.'

'But I'm seven!'

Clare saw them coming from the caravan. She immediately reminded David about the drying-up.

'Clare, I think Sheila should go to bed. She's had a long day.'

While he did the drying-up, he found a handy little kitchen knife, very sharp, and slipped it in his pocket. Clare, who had only just managed to get Sheila settled in the tent, was furious with him when he told her he was going out for a walk again.

'It'll be dark soon!' she protested. 'I don't like people walking about in the dark.'

'I won't be long.' Clare snorted her resentment, and flung herself down on her bunk.

He went down to the soft turf with its embroidery of sea-pinks and tried to count the skull heads. Even in the evening dark they were visible. There must be at least forty now, even closer than before. He supposed that was not unusual, but thought they did not come into sea-lochs like this. In a fit of fever he looked about him for stones and started to hurl jagged lumps of rock at them, yelling and shouting. His stones fell short. He advanced on to the foreshore and selected round pebbles, hurling these until his shoulder ached, cursing at the seals. They did not even move away, but on the contrary seemed to edge closer. He still could not reach them. He bawled at them wildly.

'Come in, you bastards! Come in! I'm talking to you too! Come in where I can hit you!'

He was aware he must appear mad, but it seemed desperately important for a reason he could not define. He was suddenly struck by a screaming kicking thing from behind that nearly overbalanced him into the water. It was Sheila, screeching and pummelling at him like a mad thing.

'Leave my seals alone! I hate you!' Tears were streaming down her face. 'Leave them alone. They've suffered enough!' She had her arms wrapped around his legs with such strength that he could not even move. 'If you harm them I'll kill myself! I hate you, I hate you!'

Clare came running down to the shore in her ungainly way, hobbling and hurting herself on the stones. She was white and frightened.

'What's going on? What's all the screaming?'

'Sheila flew at me . . . she lost her temper . . .'

'He was throwing stones at the seals, Mummy! Don't ever let him do that again!' The strong grip around David's legs relaxed. He was astounded by that grip. It had had the strength of a man. Clare gave David a look of fury combined with contempt. He was a murderer in their eyes. He silently wandered off to the small wood by the ruin, hearing Clare comforting the child and re-establishing her in her tent. He found a length of stout wood and trimmed off the side branches with the kitchen knife. It made a handy club. He had no idea what he was going to do with it, but if a seal came ashore, he was going to beat its brains out, as they clubbed them on the Farne islands. He wrapped the weapon in his jacket and smuggled it into the caravan like a convict. He tucked it between his bunk and the side. Clare was definitely not speaking to him anyway.

Sheila dreamed that they all came, the grey and lovely ones, gliding easily. They talked without speaking and she understood all they said simultaneously through some magic infusion of tongues. They called her name in a sibilant whisper, over and over like the soft breaking of surf on the shore. Silver fish flashed to left and right. She must join them.

The sea was green and salty. She felt the pressure upon her. It was very deep now and they urged her down, down. She knew without knowing where they wanted her to go. Barnacled walls, encrusted plates of ships. All the drowned men were smiling. Lobsters crawled through ribs and sockets. The pain will soon pass. Down, down, we have no pain. Down.

It was ten minutes past two by his watch when David was awakened by the horrible slobbering sort of noise and the soft dragging sound. He leaped from his bed, grabbing his club and charged into the darkness, treading on something cold and nauseous that made him slip. In the moonlight he saw the skull-like faces and the slithering creature that seemed to be embracing Sheila in the tent. He tore the tent down, and hit and hit at the beast's head. There was a frantic commotion all around him. The other animals were fleeing back to the loch. Sheila seemed to awake in a trance. She started to scream, at first almost a whimper, then loudly.

'It's all right!' David kept shouting. 'It's all right!' Sheila was splashed with blood. He dragged the seal away by the flippers as best he could. Clare tumbled out of the caravan, holding a torch.

'No! Put it out!' David shouted. 'It's a seal. I've killed it. It was in the tent.' He picked up Sheila. The child was white and cold.

'My God, she's hurt!'

'No. No, she's not. It's the seal. Get her warm. Dress her up.' He knew he was gabbling. 'We're getting out of here!' He tore the tent out of the ground, and flung Sheila's possessions into the back of the caravan. The black formless thing seemed still to be moving. David took a length of guy rope and noosed it about the back flippers, avoiding looking at the pulped head. He started to drag the thing down to the shore. There, watched by the unseeing eyes from the sea, he smashed and smashed at its head, bawling hysterically like a child. When he left the thing it was still making bubbling noises. Out at sea there was a sound like human crying. David was sick into a whin bush.

They drove at speed, the caravan jolting behind. The wipers slashed wildly, trying to cope with the rain. Clare sat in the back with Sheila wrapped in a blanket. The child was white and still. Clare cried openly.

'We'll get to that hotel!' David was calling, over and over again, 'We'll be all right.' He could hardly see through the rain. The headlamp beams limited his vision to a blurred white triangle with stone walls each side. He coped with a sharp bend, the caravan beginning to slide. Steering into it they got round. As the beams of light cut round in an arc, they shone full on the shepherd, in the middle of the road with his flock of sheep. He stood there with arms outstretched wide as if to welcome them in some insane gesture. David stamped on the brake, knowing it was hopeless. The car and caravan skidded violently with a noise like cloth ripping. The caravan jack-knifed, hit the bridge coping and shot forward again, taking the car with it, broadsides. With a vicious crash of masonry and metal, they both disappeared over the edge. There was a terrible pause of only a second, then a splintering smash on the rocks below. The headlamps extinguished. The night was immediately silent again, except for the hiss of the rain.

The sergeant from Mallaig had driven a long way to get there. He was leaning on what remained of the parapet with his opposite number from Glenfinnan. They were watching two constables supervising the fixing of chains to the wreckage. Both car and caravan were upside down in the burn. Beside them on the bridge, a mobile crane purred noisily. Two other constables were measuring out and plotting the tyre marks. Meikle, the man from Mallaig, was puzzled.

'He came down here, at some speed, mind, he gets round

the bend all right, then on the straight here, he brakes like a madman. Look at the length of the skid. It was pouring with rain too. Now why? There was no one here, no trace of anything.'

'Deer?' said MacIntyre from Glenfinnan.

'But he would have hit them. At that speed. We've been over the hill and there's nothing there. And you don't brake like that for a deer. I mean, ye brake, but not stand on it like that poor devil.'

'Then the caravan hits the far side, comes back and, wham, he's over the edge.'

'Aye, if it is only one. We canna get tae the back o' the car yet. Ye can see the caravan. Just broken open. Nothing there.'

'Sheep then?'

'Na, there's nae sheep hereabouts. He'd have hit them anywise.'

'Drunk?'

'That we'll need to see. Where is that bloody ambulance anyway?' There was a shout from down below. One of the constables was yelling that the chains were on. The two sergeants moved over to the raw yellow stone of the hole in the parapet. The constable made a circular motion in the air, and the crane driver revved up, with a stench of diesel blowing into the clear air. The chains tightened and the car was lifted, very slowly, out of the bed of rocks. The constable held up his hand to halt the crane. The noise died to a grumbling roar.

'Here comes the nasty bit,' said the Glenfinnan man.

'Aye.' They walked across the bridge, ready to go down the steep side into the ravine. All around them, the world seemed sweet. Gorse was heavy with bloom and linnets sang, ignoring the rumbling crane. A constable was tentatively trying to see inside the crushed wreckage. None of the doors would open. The two men reached the burn side in time to see the young constable making a dive for the bushes. The other one, very white, with reddish hair, looked as though he was about to pass out.

'All right, Jamie,' said the Mallaig man to him. 'It takes you like that. Sit down ower there and wait a bit. Me and the sergeant will see.'

'No, sergeant, it's no' that. I've seen this sort o' thing afore. I was brought up on a farm. There's a deid man in the front, but it's what's in the back. There's a woman in there.'

'Deid?'

'Aye, but Jesus Christ, she's got this seal in her arms, all dressed up in clothes! Holding it!'

In the silence that followed, they were aware of the din of the linnets in the hot sun. Bees droned about in the gorse flowers reminding the sergeant from Glenfinnan horribly of flies. The sergeant from Mallaig was of tougher stuff.

'Well, did nobody think tae call the vet?' They went down the slope together.

It was eighteen weeks before they found the body of a girl in the loch. Her skull was terribly crushed.

BELIAH

Beliah is the name of the best friend I ever had. Without him I would not be alive – I might have died in adolescence. Without Beliah I would certainly not be the kind of man I am.

He intruded into my life at a time when I had great need of friendship and succour.

I was thirteen or fourteen years old. I was staying that summer with my Uncle Timothy and his family at their country house. 'Of course he'll go,' said my mother to her neighbour. 'Let him take his white face there. Good food and plenty of exercise. He'll come back in time for the new school year brimming with health . . .'

I went, reluctantly. I had recently recovered from mumps.

My instinct, as nearly ever, was correct. I was miserable at The Howe, however good the fare and the surroundings.

My cousins, after a first brusque sounding, turned away from me one after the other. They swam in the sea; they rode ponies; they pulled each other's hair and clothes with wild screams in the garden.

I had no part in that life. I was a solitary child, who played the piano and read books.

Uncle Timothy, newly a widower, was as kind to me as a preoccupied businessman could be. 'Well, lad,' he would say, 'how goes the holiday? Are you being attended to? Sail the boat whenever you want. Good. I saw a fire down at the cave just now as I drove in. That'll be Justin and George. I'll put a stop to that – the fishermen won't like it.'

Then the gong would go for dinner, and the three of them – Justin and George and Maggie my cousins – would come rushing in (on this evening smelling of smoke, and with bits of ash in their hair).

'Why were you not at the shore?' said Maggie coldly to

me. 'We lit a fire. We jumped through it. Justin got his sleeve singed.'

I said I had been reading.

'You're a coward,' said Justin. 'You're frightened of nearly everything. You won't even dip in the sea. Why didn't you join us in the apple-tree this morning when I shouted to you to come up?'

I said nothing.

'Leave him alone,' said George. After a few brooding seconds he turned to me. 'Did you know, Hubert,' he said, 'that your bedroom is haunted? A ghost – a sailor with a harpoon-wound in his throat. He was murdered a hundred years ago. That's the room he appears in.'

They sniggered at my blanched face; then suddenly occupied themselves with the flowers in the vase or the fringe of the table-cloth, for their father was coming in from the kitchen bearing the roast lamb on a platter.

'Now, listen you,' said Uncle Timothy, 'about that fire down at the cave . . .' He lectured them ineffectively about the danger to the nets, and how the kelp gatherers wouldn't like it.

The meal ended. They rushed down to the shore, to bathe in the sunset waters.

I went on with my reading.

I was not seriously frightened about the ghost of the whaler. I had convinced myself, after the first stab of panic, that it was impossible. The big house was only ten years old; what would a century-old ghost want among all those new stylish furnishings? Ghosts wander, if anywhere, through the labyrinth of their own finished lives.

When I was lying in bed, however, I heard ghost noises in the corridor outside – a sigh, a wail, a shriek. A brief silence was followed by muffled sniggers, then a hollow threat, 'I'm coming to get you at midnight . . .' Then my three cousins dispersed, on woollen feet, to their rooms.

I began to hate them very much. But I would have to be patient under the persecution – there was a fortnight of holiday left.

That night, on the verge of sleep, I heard myself saying distinctly, 'Beliah, I'm sad here and I'm lonely and I'm very very unhappy. Help me.'

A sweet voice said, 'Play the piano. That'll put things right for you.'

I obeyed the voice, like a somnambulist.

I put on dressing-gown and slippers and went softly downstairs to the drawing-room. It was still light enough, in the heart of the northern summer, to see the keyboard and the music-sheets. Nevertheless I lit a candle, and the whole room was beautiful in that gentle wavering light.

I made the first music that came to my heart and fingers. I must have improvised for half an hour or more. In the music the truth about this house gradually disclosed itself.

I was not a lonely despised boy at all. I was a young lord in my Hall on the sea-coast. Until I came of age all my affairs were in the hands of a kind fussy anxious uncle. Every great house is full of shadows and whispers. I was aware of the envy and enmity of my cousins, but it did not touch me at all. They were mulish creatures. The kindest thing that could happen to Justin would be death in battle; in no other way would he be spoken about by the next generation. Who remembers the ugly face of a bird-tormentor? I would speak to the captain of the mercenaries about Justin . . . I would not distress a convent by putting Maggie into one, when her time came. Better that one man, and a few children like her, should suffer, than a dovecote of innocents. Those thick shoulders of hers were made for house drudgery. She would have a dowry . . . George one could do very little with. Even death in battle was out for him. He would turn tail at the first trumpet echo. Of course, being well-born and of my breed, he couldn't groom horses or mend nets. The creature was interested in the sea – what might be best for him would be to get him a ship in a few years' time, in the hope that some North Sea storm, or a skerry off Shetland, would put an end to him. (The ship would be a small price to pay.)

I rose sated from the piano stool, quenched the candle,

and went softly along the corridor to my room.

'Thank you, Beliah,' I said. 'It was good advice you gave me.'

Then I drew the quilt over my head and went to sleep.

Next morning there was trouble at the breakfast table. Uncle Timothy turned up with a flake of scarlet cotton-wool on his cheek; he had cut himself shaving. He settled himself, scowling, in the big chair at the head of the table. Marian brought in kippers and rolls.

The three cousins gave each other quick alarmed looks. Their father was usually at his best in the morning.

'You, girl,' he said to Maggie. 'What the devil do you mean by it?'

'By what?' said Maggie.

'Don't act the innocent with me!' he shouted. 'You know perfectly well what you were doing at midnight last night – making that hellish noise on the piano.'

'I have not played the piano for days,' said Maggie.

'Listen,' said Uncle Timothy, 'I am not a hard father to any of you. You have perfect freedom to do almost anything you want. I don't interfere. But I am a busy man and I have important work to do and I need my sleep. *I need my sleep.* That damn piano wakened me up round about midnight. It was four hours – *four hours* – before I dropped off again. I'm telling you this, Maggie, it's a good thing for you I never get out of bed once I'm in it, for if I had done last night I'd have thrashed you, big girl as you are and all.'

'I didn't play the piano,' said Maggie.

The look of honesty on her face convinced him. He turned his fierceness on the two boys. 'Which of you was it?' he cried. 'Own up. Tell me the truth. I'm going to stop his money for a week, whichever one it was. Speak.'

The boys shook their heads dumbly.

'Very well,' said Uncle Timothy. 'I've been a good father to you . . .' I had not thought such self-pity to be a part of him, but I understood that the man was spinning platitudes in order to think out a suitable punishment for his ungrate-

ful children. At last, among the kipper bones and the mar-
malade, sentence was pronounced. 'The boat is to be hauled
up. The boat is to be put in the shed for the rest of the
summer. That's my punishment for liars and disturbers of
the peace.'

At that, George let a wail out of him. Rills of grief
streamed down his freckled face. 'You can't do that! The
Merle's entered for the regatta on Tuesday. You can't do it,
Dad.'

'I can,' said Uncle Timothy, 'and I will.'

At this point I thought it high time to put the truth before
the household. 'Finish your breakfast in peace,' I said.
'Such melodramatics so early in the morning! It was I who
played the piano last night late.'

I have rarely seen such wonderment on four faces at one
time.

'You, Hubert?' said Uncle Timothy blankly.

'Yes, Uncle Timothy,' I said. 'I have a perfect right to
play my own piano in my own house whenever I choose.'

The looks of wonderment deepened; in the case of Justin
and George it was almost awe. Maggie, who was the most
humorous of the three, was preparing for laughter.

'It might be difficult for you to grasp,' I said. '*Must* be
difficult, impossible even for such a stupid boy as George.
The truth is, you are all living a masquerade here. I, Hubert,
am the only one who knows what's what. It would be cruel
to break your illusions yet. So you'll just go on living, meantime, in the usual way. Some day, of course, I'll remove the
disguises from you as gently as possible.'

'God,' said Maggie.

'Hubert,' said Uncle Timothy, 'are you feeling all right?
Do you think you might have a touch of fever? Maggie, put
your hand on Hubert's brow.'

'In the end,' I said, 'you will all be given your different
avocations. Justin, I think soldiering is the thing for you –
you with your punching and bullying. George, you are to be
the skipper of a ship. You see how kind I am to you, though
you all do your best to make me unhappy. Maggie, a hus-

band and children for you, in a house as far away from me as possible.'

Uncle Timothy had slipped out into the hall. He was speaking on the telephone.

'Uncle Timothy,' I called, 'I want to thank you now for all your good work on my estate. I think you've been fairly honest. Whom are you phoning?'

Justin seized me by the hair and pulled. 'You're bonkers,' he whispered. 'You're off your bloody rocker.'

Maggie kicked me under the table. Then her ugly face broke apart with merriment.

'A sudden shock,' said George. 'Let's dip him in the sea, now. Catch his legs, Maggie.'

The rest of that day, and in fact several succeeding days, I was confused in my mind. I was in bed. I remember Mrs Morris the housekeeper bending over me; and the doctor with needles and tablets; and Marian washing me. Uncle Timothy came from time to time, looking stupid and distraught. The three hated faces must have been forbidden the room.

I suffered them all, and the things they were doing to me. After all, they had to play the parts set down for them in the masquerade. I alone – though a player also – stood naked in the fire of truth.

One night Beliah came. 'Well done,' he said. 'Life, that you feared so much, is going to be a great adventure for you from now on. And I won't ever leave your side, Lord Hubert.'

I did not see Beliah – there was only the sweet voice in the darkness.

I suffered them, in the end, to take me back to my mother's house.

As the car drove out through the wide gate of The Howe, I saw the three cousins in the apple-tree. They screwed up their faces, they scratched their rumps like monkeys, they spat after the car. The girl from the next farm, Janine, had come to play with them. She was a sweet girl – she threw me a kiss and waved her hand.

My mother, that good hard-working woman, received me at the door.

'Welcome home, my dear,' she said. 'Are you feeling better now? You've been through a bad time. Well, you'll be all right now. Bless you. That mumps took more out of you than we thought.'

Later, over the dinner-table, she said, 'We can't be too thankful to your Uncle Timothy. (Eat your soup, there's a good lad, it'll make you strong.) The things he did for you – the trouble he went to! And those three dear children, how concerned they were! Now, Hubert, you're not to worry about it. It was some kind of obscure nervous trouble. The doctor tried to explain it all to me, but I'm just an ignorant old woman, I couldn't take it all in. "If the boy lives quietly," were the last words the doctor said to me, "and if he isn't upset or over-stimulated, there's no reason why he should ever have another attack like that . . ." It seems, dear, you spoke and did all sorts of strange things, as if you were living out a dream. I don't suppose you remember a single thing about it.'

I smiled and pressed her hand. In fact, my lordly robes, Beliah, the music, my utterances of truth in that delusion-ridden household, were the most pure and radiant things I had ever known.

(2)

The sea came at the boat in surge after crashing surge. The aim of the snow seemed to be to wind me in a grey cocoon. 'Keep her head into the sea,' said Alister. 'I'm doing that,' said my cousin George from the cabin. 'I think I know how to steer a boat.' Half an hour ago Janine, George's fiancée, had begun to be frightened. She said nothing, but her knuckles shone white and her eyes were fixed on a vacant corner of the cabin.

The crew of the *Jarl* were all in the wheelhouse but me.

George had ordered me inside ten minutes previously. I preferred the teeth and claws of the storm. I must have been a fearsome sight, standing up in the stern with one half of me shrouded in snow and the other side shining and salted. The sea and the blizzard were coming at us from roughly opposite quarters. But it was difficult, in that wild whirl, to tell.

'You're steering east,' said Alister.

It was to have been a visit, on Easter Monday, to an islet where an obscure miracle-working Celtic saint had lived and died in his cell. 'It was an isle,' said the saga, 'whereof the very stones had healing and heavenly joys in them . . .' George and Janine were not particularly religious, but Janine's hobby when she isn't teaching is archaeology; she wanted to see if there were any remnants left of the saint's hermitage, a shining scatter of stones on the beach. It had been a fine morning when we set out from Hamnavoe, all sun and dapplings of blue and grey on the sea. That black bruise on the horizon westward, who was to know that it would suddenly unfurl and enwrap us? The sea too began to furrow and crest and cry to the raging of the bear-blizzard. On the open Sound we were lost and compassless.

'Give me credit,' said George, 'for knowing what I'm about.'

Janine sat there in her khaki duffle-coat as if she were in a trance.

'You'll drive us straight against the crags, the way you're going,' said Alister. Alister is Janine's brother – an excise officer – a pleasant chap to have a dram with in the evening in the bar of the fishing hotel. The grey finger was on him too – it is not a good thing to see fear in a man's face.

George said nothing. He was too angry. His seamanship, his knowledge of this coast and these waters, being called into question! And yet he did not know any more than we did where we were or what direction we were sailing in. George is no hero either, but just for the minute his hurt pride left small room for terror. That would come. He held his course obstinately.

Sometimes the sky would lighten a little, and then Janine

would open her little fist and her eyes would flicker. But then the storm would come about us with thicker ravellings than ever. We were well wrapped in the bear's fleecy arms. The important thing was, where was this dance with the bear taking us?

The boat turned to starboard; she wallowed and heaved in trough after trough. Janine covered her mouth with her hand. George, on reflection, must have decided that maybe there was something in what Alister had said. The *Jarl* heaved about. She no longer smashed into the surges. The huge power of the sea hurled us on. The blizzard began to spin its webs from another airt. Every half-minute or so I had to scoop soft sleet out of my eyes.

'For God's sake, Hubert,' cried George, 'come inside! You give me the willies standing out there like the abominable snowman.'

'Pay attention to your steering,' said Alister anxiously.

Perhaps in the wheelhouse they could not hear it for the noise of the engine. To me, standing in the stern, it was unmistakable, the boom and crash of sea on a near cliff. But an experienced sailor like George ought to have known that there was danger ahead, for the *Jarl* had taken a different rhythm – a longer, shallower swoon between the waves.

I think Alister must have become aware of it, for he suddenly pushed George away from the wheel and seized it himself. The boat swung in huge trough after huge trough while the two men grappled for the wheel and the girl moaned and covered her eyes. It was as disgraceful a scene as I ever witnessed.

Through the snowflakes in my ear came, thrilling and sweet, the voice I had not heard for six years, 'Think of a poem, Hubert. That'll make things clear for you.'

I cried into the storm:

The sea put on a bear-mask, at my urging,
Danced here and there, frightening yokels
At the fair of Poseidon.
Now, Bjorn, Ursa, my good friend,

Your mouth and paws are a weariness at last.
I will lead you home with this halter now.
I have a pot of honey for you.
Sleep in your cave all next winter, Bjorn.

The lines became a spell that changed everything. I was an explorer earl, in quest of new fair lands to enrich my northern domain. An unheard-of thing had happened: because the weather had worsened, perhaps because there were maggots in their sea biscuits, there were murmurs and questionings and dark syllables of mutiny in the well of the ship.

I entered the great cabin. 'If you please,' I said to the entangled Alister and George, stepping over them. I took the wheel and swung the ship round. It was not a moment too soon. A bright fissure opened to starboard. We saw, enormous and spectral, the high line of cliffs towards which we had been driving.

'Go back to your duties,' I said to the crew. 'I will deal with you later. I will have to consider whether it is a hanging matter. Lady, the worst is over. You may give us the sweetness of your face again.'

By now the snow-cloud was breaking up all around us. Fissures, clefts, chasms of brightness appeared here and there, and shifted, and widened. The sun, a pale pearl, drove through the clouds, and vanished, and then stood naked in a blue pool of sky; it drenched us with light and warmth. Here and there the sea glittered.

'We will leave the discovery of that "terra nova" for another day,' I said. 'We are bound for harbour and home. Lady, I apologize for the behaviour of the cowardly crew. Your own fair eyes will witness their punishment.'

Alister and George, looking very sheepish – but red in the face still, were sitting on the bench on the opposite side of the cabin to Janine. She would not look at them. Instead she got to her feet and came and stood beside me at the wheel. The *Jarl* was crashing into the sea, through blue-and-silver cascades, like a royal steed.

The enchanted snow-bear shrank away northwards.

Half-an-hour later we entered the harbour of Hamnavoe.

We were all tired from the buffeting of the storm. After the *Jarl* was secured at her mooring, George and Alister got into the car at the pierhead without saying goodbye to me. Janine lingered. She took my hand and said, 'Thank you, Hubert,' and then was peremptorily summoned by George.

'Some day,' I said to her, 'you will know the truth about me.'

At home, my mother ran a hot bath and put two hot-water bottles in my bed.

'You'll catch your death!' she said. 'You'll get your tea in bed too. Here now, drink this at once – it's whisky and hot water.'

I drowsed in that cave of delicious warmth, my bed Before I slept I had the gratitude to say, 'Thank you, Beliah.' And Beliah whispered, 'Hubert, I was disappointed in you this morning, going to that saint's island. Places like that are hateful and hurtful to me. I had half a mind to let you drown with the others. I do not like that Janine. I think she may cause difficulties. I have plans for you, Hubert. The greatest things are to come.'

'I'm sorry, Beliah,' I said. 'Thank you.'

Then the red petals drifted on feet, hands, ears, eyes, mouth.

I was in bed with pleurisy for three weeks after that storm. I went back thinner and more silent to the loom that hid me, until my time came, from the ignorant world.

(3)

I know nothing about Beliah; where he comes from, what his status is – though I can guess.

I had been an imaginative child, but there was nothing to nourish the imagination in our house. The only books my father had were religious works. There was a piano in the parlour; I learned to play it, but it could only be opened for accompanying psalms and hymns. My father was angry one day when I dared to play some fragment of *The Messiah*. It might be thought that there could be delight in the loom in my father's shop. No such thing – a monotonous regular output of squares of tweed, all of the same size, all of the drabbest shades of grey and green. I imagined magical things happening in that clacking loom. I promised myself that when I came into the business the weaver's shop would be an exciting place. Not while my father lived; every morning he went gloomily from the breakfast table back among his webs of grey and green, and came in again at five o'clock, tired and stuck here and there with bits of wool. Then the long prayer before tea.

He died when I was eleven; then my mother had to carry on the business herself. Three years later, when I left school, I was able to help her. Already I knew the rudiments of the trade.

Among the dreary books in the parlour cupboard had been one about hell and its princes and potentates. It was an ancient book, with eighteenth-century type and illustrated with crude wood-cuts. I lingered over this book with fascination and dread, and slowly sipped the black honey. There were pictures and 'biographies' of all the devils, from Satan downwards. One of them, I remember, was called Belial. I stared long into that proud dark perverted face.

This Beliah, my dark angel and comforter, is he Belial – with the slight change that a child might make with his immature pronunciation and flawed memory? I could not conceive that such a great devil would go to all that trouble on behalf of any human being, even a lord in disguise. Still, my friend (I told myself) might well be one of Belial's host, a minion set on earth from time to time to remind me of what I truly was. Or perhaps he never left my shoulder, and in silence watched my ripening.

'What book does that boy read night after night?' said my father one winter evening.

'I don't know,' said my mother mildly. 'Ask him.'

I held the warped and must-smelling volume out.

'This is not for you,' said my father, and put it in his pocket. 'There are other more wholesome books in the house. Read them.'

I never saw that book again. I think my father must have put it in the fire. It was not among his papers after he died, though I searched long and diligently.

Is this all that Beliah is, a whisper in my ear on scant occasions when I am driven into a corner by fear, or loneliness, or delight? If he exists at all, why doesn't he come and speak to me at other times, when I am at the loom or fishing for trout in the tranquil loch on a summer evening? Why does he choose to remain invisible always?

I believe I did see him once.

Every year in late summer a troop of fairground people visited the islands. They set up their tents and booths in a field outside the town. Then, for several nights on end, their loudspeakers blared and the town children ran with candy-floss, goldfish, and twittering birds made of coloured wood-shavings.

One evening, after I had put the shutters up, I strolled out to the fairground. It was the last night of the shows; the field swarmed with hundreds of merry-makers. Whisky bottles were offered and tilted. The swing-boats cut arcs against the darkening sky. The merry-go-round revolved with shrieks and tinny music. There were coconut shies and rifle-shooting booths and the veiled tent of the fortune-teller decorated with cats and planets. I saw also the closed tent of Zorba, the Nubian Prince – 'Iron can't wound him! Fire can't burn him! Come In and See – Admittance 6 pence.'

A small Jewish-looking cigar-smoking man stood on a platform in front of a marquee and issued challenges to the crowd on behalf of his three boxers who stood, dressing-gowned and broken-nosed, beside him. Nobody responded. The manager threw doubts on the manhood of the locals. He was answered with jeers and laughter.

I turned away after half an hour. I remember thinking, 'Here it is, life in microcosm – a strut and a fret – a world rigged out in coloured rags to hide the sordidness and stupidity of it all . . .'

At the edge of the crowd I almost ran into a stranger, a young Negro. You know how it is: you step aside to give the on-comer room, he steps in the same direction; the same antic is at once, and simultaneously, performed by both parties in the opposite way; and in the end you are all but entangled with your opposite.

This is what happened between myself and the fairground man. We smiled, touched each other lightly, murmured an apology, went our opposite ways. Five paces beyond me he turned and said, 'Good night.'

I have never heard the simple valediction uttered with such sweetness and power. It halted me in my steps. It was a voice I had heard before, at certain crises in my life – Beliah's dark musical whisper.

The crowd was closing round the stranger. I tried to follow him, but was stuck like a fly in honey. I had time to glimpse him dodging into the tent of Prince Zorba.

As I left the fairground a voice came through a megaphone. 'On show now! Zorba the mystic African prince! Price sixpence . . .' But I could not bring myself to watch this noble friend of mine licking red-hot pokers with his tongue and lying down on a bed of nails . . .

Next morning the field was empty but for a wide strewment of tinsel and cardboard and empty bottles. The fair had packed and gone.

I would have gone down to the pier in the hope of seeing once more that black enchanting presence; but overnight some virus had got into me, and I was in bed for ten days, pallid and drugged. Each encounter with Beliah seemed to drain all the health out of me.

My mother said, 'Never did I hear such nonsense out of any human mouth! What dreams you must have been having! I swear, Hubert, I was frightened sometimes, just listening to you!'

(4)

My mother, one of two sisters, married 'beneath her'. Their father, last survivor of an old Norse family, cultivated a large farm ten miles from Hamnavoe. The elder daughter, Emma, married Timothy Strange, a successful merchant and businessman, and they had the three cousins whose torments first took Beliah into my life.

My mother married the unprosperous evangelical weaver. I was their only child. (Or rather, this is my pedigree as it *appears* to be in registrar's ledger, in record office, in popular acceptance. The truth, as we know, is far otherwise.)

I do not for one moment believe that I am son of the weaver and this woman who feeds me and sees to all my wants. No matter though people say, 'How like your mother you are!' – no matter that the mirror flashes back her looks and expressions at me – 'My soul has had elsewhere its setting', and that setting was princely.

Often enough I fretted, in my workshop, over the low disguise I was forced to wear. How much longer would it be until the truth was made known openly to the world? I possessed my soul with as much patience as I could. In the meantime I did a little to make my durance less vile. For one thing, new and striking designs began to issue from the loom. The whole colour spectrum was evoked, with all its subtle shadings and blendings. I learned to weave like the medieval web-men; and I brought to my work a little of their dedication and scrupulousness.

My work was very much admired by certain visitors and tourists. I did a good business during the holiday season. I was given commissions that kept me busy most of the winter.

Hardly a visitor ever came to our house. In my father's day a few glum preaching-men would gather in the parlour at the weekend. After he died even they stopped coming. My mother and I lived in almost complete solitude. I have never been interested in other people. The only exception was Janine; she would call on us sometimes when her husband George was on one of his long sea-trips. For Janine alone I felt a kindness and sympathy; we murmured mildly to each other like shells on a shore. I have always hated physical contact. Janine and I would touch hands whenever anything excited us or intrigued us. We even signed out meetings and departures with small cold kisses. Sometimes, thinking of her, I was eaten up with envy. Why had I not been born ordinary and good-hearted like her? She would go with her honest troubled face among my weavings. 'They're good, Hubert. Very good. But there's something I don't like about them – an unwholesomeness – a shadow ... I don't know what it is ... I can't explain it ...'

'You are not to worry, Janine,' I would say, 'about the mysteries of art. There's my mother calling. The tea-pot's on the stove ...'

I suppose, if I had been an ordinary craftsman, I would have been happy enough – especially in the knowledge that I had transformed a drab place into a gallery strewn with rich strange things. But more and more, as the years passed, I longed to come into my true inheritance. A darkness, that lasted for days, would enwrap my mind. Most folk, in these circumstances, would have bought a tonic from the chemist-shop or gone away for a holiday. I applied myself to my work with redoubled intensity. Nor, for five years, did I have one word of comfort or advice from the friend and guardian.

It came, unexpectedly, one morning in midsummer.

I had been commissioned by no less a person than my cousin Justin to do a tapestry incorporating his family 'coat-of-arms'. I do not think such a thing existed outside Justin's fly-blown imagination. Still, I accepted his sketch and promised delivery at the month's end.

I was at that time enduring a most utter darkness and desolation of the spirit.

The spurious coat-of-arms consisted of a shield with a red rose on one half and a dagger on the other. I worked a whole day and half a night on the rose. There issued, in spite of my soul-sickness, a vivid piece of work (though how such a fragrant symbol could ever have blossomed on a family tree that contained Justin and George and Maggie was more than I could imagine). When the rose was finished I felt utterly prostrated – I knew I could not work any more that night. As if to emphasize the decision, my candle gulped and went out and left me in darkness.

It came then, a single syllable, but it was all music and all release and delight – 'Weave.'

'I will, friend,' I said. 'It's a long while since I heard from you. Bide a little, now that you're here.'

He remained, but wordless, while I made haste to re-light the tall thick candle and arrange my wools. Before morning I had woven the black dagger into the tapestry. I looked, and saw that the work was a portent and a summons.

After breakfast I got into my car and drove the ten miles to The Howe. The finished work lay rolled on the seat beside me.

There in the garden (for it was a beautiful Sunday morning) sprawled my Uncle Timothy, half-asleep in a deck chair. Maggie, who looked after the house now (she was not yet married but was engaged to a purple-faced farmer) was weeding the garden. There was no sign of Justin. George was home from sea; he would likely be sleeping off his Saturday-night binge. I thought, with a pang, of Janine lying there beside him.

Here and there on the road a few country folk were making for the church down at the shore. I entered the garden. My good steward (but why had he kept me from my inheritance so long?) had opened one eye at the squealing of the gate ... 'Oh, hullo,' said she coldly who had the housekeeping of this great hall of mine, with all its many chambers and annexes, wells and larders and fires.

'Come in, Hubert. You're welcome, man,' cried Uncle Timothy.

'Address me as "my lord",' I said. I took my mother's bread-knife from the enfolding tapestry. Then I stabbed the

kind old man six or seven times. I almost laughed at the look
of utter astonishment on his face.

'Well done,' said Beliah's voice out of the blackberry
bush. 'Oh, that was good, man!'

Maggie began to scream from the other side of the garden.

Roses blossomed here and there on the white shirt of the
dying man.

(5)

I have been in this high tower now, a prisoner, for thirty-
five years.

Thirty-five years exiled from my inheritance, and just
when I thought I had opened the door into it. Meantime, the
indignities of age have crept upon me – greyness, toothless-
ness, rheumatism, diminishing sight, querulousness.

The blackest thing of all is the loneliness of my prison.
Visitors indeed come from time to time; but never once, in
all that great stretch of time, the friend I long for, he who
infused such sweetness and power and mystery into my
youth. I must face it – I can hardly expect to come into my
own now, this side of death. The consummation is to be in
eternity. Then I will see my friend face to face. My hand
trembles as I write – I can hardly wait for that kiss, for that
delicious robe of darkness to be put on me.

When I say 'high tower' and 'inheritance' I speak with the
kind of stylization that is a part of me, and at the same time
a masque of the truth. For 'high tower' understand 'criminal
asylum' – that's what everybody else calls this place of my
withering.

I was arrested and in due course tried for the murder of
Timothy Strange, my uncle. The trial did not interest me at
all, except for its vestiges of ceremony. I was found guilty,
and sentenced to death. Beliah stood behind me in the dock;
he turned those dreadful words into a blessing. 'Soon we
will be together now,' he whispered.

I saw only one known face in the crowded courtroom,
Janine. Her look of grief pierced me through and through,

it was so beautiful, like a face in a stained-glass Pietà –
Magdalen's or Martha's.

The sentence was commuted to life imprisonment in a
criminal asylum. My long exile began.

Why did my guardian never come with comforting words
as the slow shadows of time began to cluster about me? I
have often thought about it. It may be that Beliah resents
this long interval before our meeting. He had looked for an
early tryst after a hanging. He comes to my room from time
to time, though, always at night. I am aware of his silent
invisible presence. I wake up with a feeling of delight, as if I
and the darkness were slowly feasting on one another, and
pledging one another, and making promises. But I long for
my ear to be ravished with his music.

(The truth of my situation is that I was captured by a king,
either of Sweden or Denmark. The ships came out of the east
suddenly, black wings against the dawn. I was down at the
shore hunting otters that morning when I was seized. My hall
was looted and burned. I was taken, blindfold, across the
sea to a castle on a rock, and lodged in the high tower, with
a chain at my ankle. I have waited a long time for the ran-
som money to be paid. My captors have waited so long the
wonder is they haven't cut my throat long ago and dropped
me into the sea. In fact they treat me with consideration and
kindness.)

The staff here look on me not so much as a patient but as
an old benign uncle who is slowly withering into dotage and
death. They know a part of my secret, I think. One of the
young doctors keeps calling me 'my lord . . .' 'And how is
your lordship this fine day?' he says, taking my wrist to feel
the pulse. 'Your lordship continues in excellent health. I
think only a bullet will put an end to such a strong man as
you, my lord . . .'

There is a communal lounge at the heart of the huge dwell-
ing. I never go there when it is full of patients, for lectures
or concerts or sermons. Sometimes, late, a nurse will take
my arm and lead me downstairs; there, for an hour, I will
play the piano, and sleep soundly afterwards.

I was asked, in the early days, to take a class in weaving.
I refused. I don't want to associate with these ordinary
lunatics.

Since the slow failing of my sight I can't read so much as
formerly. That is a great deprivation. Once or twice a week
one of the nurses will read to me, preferably out of the Norse
medieval Sagas. They do their best, but they ruin those cold
surges of prose.

I spoke of visitors. In the early days the week was studded
with them. Hardly an afternoon passed without this relative
or that acquaintance turning up. Pure curiosity attracted
some – to gawp for half an hour at a murderer and a madman. Even Justin my cousin came once in his major's uniform. It was to tell me that George his brother had been lost
at sea. What (he said anxiously) was to be done with The
Howe? Janine didn't want to go on living there. Maggie was
married to a farmer in another island and had four children.
Justin didn't like giving up the family place. I said to Major
Strange, 'I give you leave to sell The Howe. The money is to
be given to the poor . . .' He left very soon after that, bolt-
eyed.

There is one visitor who comes regularly once every year.
These visits of Janine are (besides the rare mute manifesta-
tions of Beliah) the only true joys of my exile. It may be that
Janine and I have always loved each other a little. For no
other creature have I this ache of tenderness. We don't speak
much. She knows something, I'm sure, about my divided
life. She is troubled by it, of course. But the sweet anxious
looks she puts on me, the kindness of her when she takes my
hand in hers! 'All will be well with you, Hubert,' she says. 'I
pray for you night and day. God bless you . . .' Then, after
a time, she kisses me and goes away. I will not see her again
for a year, when she comes to stay with her cousins in the
south for a holiday.

After these annual visits from Janine, I have always a
tormented night. Beliah is displeased with me. He has never
liked Janine.

It is easy enough for you, I suppose, to concur with the establishment and say, 'The man is mad.' So, in a sense, I am; I wouldn't deny it. But what is this madness that afflicts me? It is more than a wrenched and distorted psyche. We only dimly understand the workings of mind and spirit, and how time is woven into us. Individual time is not just a matter of birth to death; then the story is told, the tapestry is finished. Past and future can intrude into a man's life in mysterious potent ways. Religion and art are more aware of these intrusions and contradictions than the cold scientists of the mind who minister to me here. These are deep waters. I have gone among them often in my exile of thirty-five years. It seems to me that my essential being is held in some half-legendary caul or loop of time; a lesser 'I' is living, exiled and poor, in the twentieth century. Beliah has been striving since my adolescence to sunder the lord from the exile; it can only be done gradually; and the divorce is to be – if the few experiments as between Beliah and me are anything to go by – a difficult, dangerous, magical procedure.

But the delusion of grandeur (you might insist) – the conviction of a poor tradesman that he is a medieval lord – surely that is clear matter of madness.

Believe me, on this kind of 'madness' all Western religion is based. We are creatures fallen from high serene timeless places. Wretched and death-bound as we are, we are still heirs to those halls and diamonds and ecstasies. Who is mad then, I who have always known this, or you who are content with your seventy miserable years of 'getting and spending'?

Art too, in all its forms, seeks always to make a harmony of our manifold sunderings. Creation to the artist is a half-ruined web. In whatever form he works he seems to share in the labour of the original creator, by a patient restoring of the erosions of moth and rust. He recreates ancient lost gracious rites. He interprets the seeming chaos of his own times by these touchstones and archetypes. This is the artist in his classical role, calm, undoubting, measuring man against nature and the divine. This art, at its highest, sees immortality in the most ordinary people and actions: 'human face divine' . . . 'men, coming and going on the earth' . . . 'what glorious shapes are those?' . . . There is another kind of artist. This one storms his way into wholeness by ecstasy and incantation and fire – dark dangerous ways. He achieves his end not by the patient miracles of design but by something that can only be called magic. Other men and women are not precious immortal creatures to him; they are mere objects; he will destroy them if they come between him and his destiny. What kind of art is this? Where does it have its origin? What is its function?

Many a lonely night I pondered these matters, and was still awake when the breakfast trollies began to trundle along the corridor.

Janine came to see me yesterday. She is old like myself now, but she brings all the fresh delights of April into my room.

We exchanged our bits of news, and laughed a little; the silences were easy and kind.

I had gathered, from things she had said over the years, that Janine had become interested in religion. Her allusions to the subject were incidental, and so I had never been able to establish whether she was Presbyterian, Catholic or Zen Buddhist. Nor, truth to tell, did I care one way or the other.

Yesterday she said, 'I got to the island at last, Hubert. The sun shone all the way. It was at Easter. I found a few stones.'

'What island?' I asked.

She reminded me of the storm that day forty-five years ago. Then I remembered vividly – that had been one of my great days, a shining thread in the legend of the lord Hubert.

'You remember,' said Janine, 'the story of the devil-possessed man who was brought to the saint?'

I began to recite the saga fragment. I have (as you have no doubt guessed) a remarkable memory.

' "Holveig of Njalsay's oatfield ripened early that year. Holveig ordered his men to get the scythes out of the barn.

While the reaping was in progress, Holveig stood on the edge
of the rig. Suddenly Holveig cried out and ran into the field.
He seized a scythe from one of the harvesters and gave the
man a deep neck wound with it, so that he died that same
day. Then Holveig turned on the other men. A few of them
got cuts and wounds before he was finally overpowered.
Holveig lay all that night in his own Hall, bound and raging.
In the morning, led by a priest, Holveig's men carried their
master down to a small boat. They hoisted a sail and steered
towards the island of the saint. Holveig whimpered and
tossed in his bonds all the way. The holy man met them on
the beach. At sight of him Holveig screamed louder than
before. 'Our lord Holveig is very dear to us,' said Blan the
steward. 'Will you help him, for God's charity?' It was said
the saint had lived so long in solitude that he had forgotten
language. Now he pointed to a large flat stone that was
there. He seemed to be telling them to lay Holveig on the
stone. Then he waded out to a rock that was there and
dropped his line into the flood. 'When the tide turns,' said
Blan, 'we will take our poor lord home again. We asked this
uncharitable saint for a blessing and all he has given us is a
stone.' Holveig on his stone bed was now howling more
wretchedly than ever. His eyes bulged and he curled his lip
like a hound. Then he seemed to go to sleep briefly. When he
opened his eyes he said to his men, 'Where are we? How do
we come to be in this poor place? Why are my wrists and
feet tied? I have had a terrible dream, in which I seemed to
be in the fires of hell. This is a hard bed. Blan, good friend,
take the rope from me.' Then they unbound their lord. The
saint waded ashore soon carrying two fish. He gave one fish
to Holveig. When Holveig and his men were getting into
their boat they saw the demon that had been in Holveig go
like a cormorant across the water westward. Holveig lived
fifty years after that in health of mind and body" . . .'

That was the story that both Janine and I knew well. We
smiled at the quaint artistry of the medieval story-teller, who
had probably been a monk in some grey island, Papay or
Eynhallow.

Soon it was time for Janine to go.

The door had hardly shut behind Janine when a storm of
terror and rage and obscenity burst about my head. For the
first time in thirty-five years Beliah spoke. I recognized, and
did not recognize, the voice. 'That woman! That bitch! You
fool! Why do you ever allow the creature in? I've never
liked her, Hubert. She's dangerous. She hates me! She wants
to separate us! She can never do it – we're bound to each
other. Yes, we are! Make no mistake about that. Do you
know what she's done? You poor old blind idiot. DO NOT
TOUCH THE THING SHE LEFT ON YOUR TABLE. I forbid it! This
is what you'll do, Hubert – now listen to me – ask the nurse
when she comes in with your supper to take *the thing* out,
anywhere away from here. Hubert, touch it and everything's
over between us! Touch it and there's no pain on earth like
the suffering you'll have. I'm warning you. That old hag!
You and the hag smirking and ogling at each other! It's
disgusting. You killed her father-in-law – remember that.
Remember the courage and the beauty that you had that
day, Hubert. You idiot, go to bed – no, not yet awhile, you
must tell the nurse about the object on your table!'

There was silence for a while – my friend had exhausted
himself in his paroxysm of rage.

When he spoke again, it was the old alluring thrilling
honeyed whisper. 'I'm sorry, Hubert. Forgive me. Dear old
friend, it was a spasm of jealousy. Forget it. Forget everything but the marvellous times we've had together. Hubert,
I'm in love with you. Hubert, I can't wait till we throw our
arms about each other. The cloak of death – flames and
darkness. A short time only, dear. Then we'll be with each
other for ever.'

The seductive whisper faded. When Beliah spoke again,
there was an element of pleading in his voice.

'Don't do it,' he said, his voice lucent with tears. 'For my
sake, Hubert – your dearest friend. I was always kind to you.
I gave you gifts, didn't I? – Courage, and power, and delight. Answer me. Why are you not speaking to me, Hubert?'

From the kitchen downstairs came the rattling of plates and the tinkle of cutlery. In ten minutes, or less, Nurse McGregor, that pleasant girl, would come along the corridor with the suppers.

The cell was full of urgent words again. I had never imagined that there could be such vulgarity in immortal utterance. 'That old tart! Do you imagine that a thing like that on your table will save you, man? It's so pathetic. Listen, you. I was warned about you, right at the start. I was told. "The chances are," they said, "Hubert will rat on you in the end" . . . But you can't, you fool. The bond is signed and sealed. I have you. You'll never escape.'

The doors of the lift squeaked open. Supper trollies began to be pushed down this corridor and that. My night nurse opened the first door at the far end of our corridor.

The voice came again, tired but practical. 'When Nurse McGregor comes in with your supper, Hubert, you will say to her, "Nurse, somehow a stone seems to have been left by somebody on my table. Would you take it out, please, at once? Thank you . . ." Just say that, Hubert, and nothing is changed between us. You will still be the lord Hubert, a hero out of his age and time, an artist, a magician, an immortal!'

Another door opened and closed along the corridor. Nurse McGregor greeted another delusion-ridden one.

'Touch the stone,' said Beliah, 'and you will touch "reality", or what the ignorant of all ages think "reality" is. That kind of truth will kill you, man. You won't see morning! I have kept you all your life from such things as remorse, terror, pity. Touch the stone, and those same angels will change you into an old poor pathetic deluded dying creature. Hubert, a nurse has to shave you, your hand shakes so much. You know that, don't you? You dribble at every orifice, Hubert. You've begun to smell this past year or two . . .' He suddenly howled as if I had actually touched the stone, 'YOU WILL BE RAVAGED IN FIRES OF GRACE!'

I heard Nurse McGregor in the next ward. 'Good evening,' came her cheerful voice to the looney who had strangled his sweetheart and then buried her in his garden. 'Is it cocoa tonight, or tea, or milk?'

Beliah was weeping. Outside the eaves dripped. The whole earth was drenched with the grief of Beliah. He wept inside me. I felt his marvellous tears on my face.

THE FOOTHOLD

'Yes, you'll need to get every one of those boots and shoes back in their boxes before you've another on your hands,' said the manageress who had come down to find the havoc on the ground floor and to hear the reason for it. 'That was the sort who doesn't know his own mind, never will know it, and wouldn't buy a shoelace even if he did. Turning up at closing-time and expecting all heaven and earth!'

The young man, Thomas, still new to the job, stared at a floor littered with shoes – shoes with their heels together and wide-opened feet, boots flung in a Cossack dance of inturned toes and parted heels, some drawn up stiffly in pairs as if on parade, and all the rest stranded, the one from the other, in distant corners or washed up on their sides in waves of blue and white tissue paper. This was the way his young customer had abandoned them, mixing wildness with neatness, satisfied with none – as utterly unsatisfied as it was possible for a man to be with a shoe.

Thomas picked them all up, put them in their boxes and piled them on the shelves. He straightened the chairs and stools, replaced the foot-measures and the shelf ladders. His own feelings were mixed. The man had been more than restless. He'd had the look of one who would always be desperate to be off, no matter where or how, with new shoes on his feet or without. It corresponded more or less to his own view of things. To Thomas no part of the present could ever be right. He looked ahead. Along with annoyance went a touch of fellow-feeling for his customer.

'It puts people off to see the place like a jumble sale,' said Miss Borthwick. 'Naturally I have to remind you of certain things if I'm to go on holiday knowing the place is all right. I want to enjoy myself. I want to have peace of mind!'

'But I hope you do,' said Thomas. Everyone hoped Miss Borthwick would find peace of mind and that some residue

of it would penetrate the place from top to bottom on her
return.

On Thursday she left. Holidays had already taken one
man from the place. Thomas had now sole charge of the
men's shoes while a Mrs Kirk and the young girl, Julia,
dealt with the women and children on the floor above.
Thomas enjoyed the new freedom in the place. He was
interested in every person who came in and had been from
the start.

'That's only because you don't intend to stay,' said Mrs
Kirk, 'filling in time until better turns up. If you had to do
it month after month, year after year, it would be different.
You can afford to be interested.' This question was often
discussed in a friendly enough way – how the restless or the
lucky ones moved on. How others got stuck for life. Thomas
gave every sign of being restless. Even when putting back
shoes he had a way of looking into the empty spaces between
boxes as though they were so many escape holes through
which one of these days he might easily pass. In the opinion
of the others he hadn't the staying power for the job. He
was knocked out by a heavy day. When it came to the bit
all he had was a good ear.

It was true that Thomas had his own peculiar kind of
patience, and perhaps because he meant to be off so soon he
listened well. He listened as though each particular shoe was
on his own foot: the walking shoe, for instance, which
– with a mere stroll to the door and back – began to press
upon a toe with all the fiery hell that leather could exact
from flesh, the fashionable boot which let the toes spread
and relax while raising instant, scorching blisters at the heel.
He had to show that nevertheless he liked shoes himself and
that his faith in a happy future life for feet could endure
through all the cruel ordeals of fitting.

This particular afternoon in late autumn was no exception. He was busy until twenty minutes before closing-time
and during the last hour he had to listen to the longest stories
of the day. The last man out claimed to have climbed all the
mountains of the north-west in a pair of old plimsolls until

the arches of his feet had fallen utterly and finally. He not only wanted support for his arches. He also demanded moral support for the worthiness of the plimsoll venture. Thomas was condemned for refusing this and loudly cursed for offering advice in its stead. Not long before him a courteous old man had come in looking for slippers to replace the pair that had gone with him into hospital. One slipper had dropped off while he was being trundled along between wards and – though every lift and corridor was searched – was never seen again. He was home now with three gallstones in a pillbox and one soft slipper and he wanted, if possible, an identical pair, to have three handy in case of other accidents. He found it unbelievable that five minutes later, here, in the last shop of all, identical slippers were found, and found to fit.

A lull came after five o'clock – not only inside the shop itself but along the few yards of pavement outside and even in the air directly over it, as though a gap had opened at that spot in preparation for a new idea – the idea of night. Yet in some respects it was still the busiest time of the day. Some distance away on the north–south motorway the subdued but steady roll of lorries could be heard. On the other side of the street last-minute shoppers were crowding out of a butcher's shop and further up on the same side the homebound bus queue was growing longer every second. But now, here and there over the whole town, the gaps of night were opening.

Thomas went into the small room at the end of his department and plugged in an electric kettle. It was not much more than a curtained-off partition but it had a small table, a chair called easy in relation to the hard ones outside, and in the corner a washbasin with a roller towel and a sliver of cracked soap. Old shoe-shelves belonging to a former shop were still here but someone had now put bowls of bulbs on them, a teapot and some cups. There was also a shabby manual of First Aid, a couple of paperback thrillers and the first volume of an Encyclopaedia, A–Bamboccio. Thomas switched off the kettle and heard, through a declining sigh

of bubbling water, the bell of the outside door. He parted
the curtains and looked out. The line of back-to-back chairs
was empty, but over in the far corner, scanning the shelves
was a young man. There was no mistaking the long, narrow
back in the brown jacket. At once Thomas recognized his
customer who, a few days before, had been prepared to dis-
card shoes by the dozen. He was not only scanning boxes.
Sometimes as he moved quickly along he would touch one,
even shift it a little to look behind. 'Can I help you?' said
Thomas loudly from between the curtains. It was a phrase
which never failed to irritate independent searchers for
shoes. Thomas himself had a scunner at it. He seldom uttered it. Yet it had its uses. This particular customer however
either missed the ironic note or was stubborn to a degree.
'Can I help?' said Thomas again coming quickly forward
through the shop, for several boxes now had their lids off.
The young man turned without hurry, quietly bringing his
hands down to his sides. For a second time that week they
faced one another. Again Thomas saw the oval head, the
pale, Modigliani face, egg-shaped above the long neck. A
blue shirt opened back from collarbones as sharp as winter
twigs. The wrists were long, the ankles thin – Thomas remembered for he had seen these ankles. The pale brown hair
was smooth as a cap – and combed or perhaps blown that
way – it formed a sleek little cone on top of his head. His
look was neither hostile nor friendly. He waited. If Thomas
had felt some sympathy before, this time his heart sank. A
second time round could bring more awkward things to
light. It was nothing about the man, he told himself. But it
was late. Time to be home.

'Can you – *can* you help?' said the young man suddenly.
The trite phrase was echoed with such deadly seriousness
that Thomas was silent for a moment while a pair of intent
eyes searched his own.

'I can simply show you more or less what I showed you
last time,' he said. 'You weren't, if you remember, very
pleased with our stock. But I can bring them all out again,
and one or two more if that's what you want to see.' The

man moved to a chair and quickly untied the laces of his shoes. Thomas went to the shelves and began to look for the eights in walking shoes. He felt as he shifted boxes and opened lids that this was not only a repeat of the time before, but that he could be almost certain the outcome would be the same. The difference lay in himself. He had long ago made up his mind that at five-thirty on the dot the place would be shut up, the CLOSED placard hung on the door.

'But we measured you last time,' he said when he'd climbed down, his arms full of shoes, to find the young man with his foot already on the slanting board and sliding the rule towards his big toe.

'To make sure,' murmured the other. He took one shoe from the pair Thomas offered and examined it carefully, turning it over to look at the sole and sliding his hand inside before trying it on. But almost before his heel was in he shook his head.

'But tie it up first!' said Thomas. More vigorously the customer shook his head, returning it to the floor with one sharp kick of his foot. He tried the buckled shoes after the laced ones, the plastic shoes after the expensive leathers, the black and tan suedes and brown pigskins. All these he rejected.

It was two minutes past the half-hour. Mrs Kirk and Julia had come down together from the floor above and were now standing at the door looking out into the street. They were not worried about locking up. They shared this with Thomas on alternate nights. They were discussing whether it was worth putting up umbrellas for the first few drops of rain. Mrs Kirk with a hairset to preserve decided for it. Thomas watched them making quickly for the bus-stop, Mrs Kirk now separated from her companion by a deep, transparent umbrella which came almost down to her waist. Thomas missed their company. Usually all three would stand and talk at the door. Tonight they had not given one backward glance down the long shop.

'You tried those buckled ones before. They were too

large,' said Thomas. 'But the first pair looked good. The fit
was right. Try them again. I have them in black as well as
with a slightly more built-up heel. If you'd care to try . . .'

'Oh, it is not the shape, the cut, the colour!' cried the
young man. 'It is ease, *ease* I'm after!' Taken aback,
Thomas stared down at him. Yet what was unnerving about
this cry? Much the same plea could be heard a dozen, dozen
times a day in the place. The brand-names of shoes spelt
ease. The posters promised it. Day in day out the problem
of comfort was thrashed out between these walls, moving
through ardent will-to-believe to downright scepticism. Yet
how different was this cry – wrung from a heart and not a
foot. Its force was such that Thomas exclaimed with feeling:
'You'll get it. I can promise you that.'

'Don't think I'll give up, for I will not,' answered the
young man. 'Oh I WILL NOT!' Thomas took a step back,
breathing quickly. Quickly he resumed the salesman role.
'Then try other places,' he said. 'You've seen our stuff and
I can't help you. You'll find other shoes, no doubt – better
shoes for your walks.'

'Walks!' cried his customer instantly. 'Do you call it that?
The never-ending, never-resting plod. The ceaseless, useless
search!' He had the loose, buckled shoe on one foot and as
he leant forward he kicked it off with such violence that it
flew up towards the far corner and landed soft as a cat on
the rug at the foot of the stairs. 'Walks!' he exclaimed with
a softer scorn.

Thomas had not turned round. He sat leaning forward,
one elbow on his knee, his chin in his hand. His customer
sat back in his chair with his eyes half-closed. A passer-by
seeing them might imagine they had a problem to solve.
A chessboard would have seemed more fitting between them
than the foot-rest. It was very still inside the shop, but now
and then there came a tentative needle-prick of rain at the
windows. 'I am closing the shop,' said Thomas quietly,
making no move but looking obliquely past the feet of his
customer. 'Don't, please, come back. There's nothing for you
here. If it's shoes you want they'd better be made to measure.

Go to someone who'll help – someone who knows the problem.'

'*You* will help,' said the young man, bending close. '*You* know the problem. You too are restless. Rootless. You are unfixed. Footloose you call it. Already malcontent.' A grimace drew the mouth down. 'You long to be, perhaps, – a free spirit!'

Thomas sprang to his feet and went quickly to the shelves, grabbing up shoe boxes on the way. He pitched them in wherever there were spaces. Sizes and colours went by the board. He was noisy about it as he dragged the short ladder around with him, but he spoke only once to the figure in the centre of the room, 'No, no, I am not restless, not discontented,' he said as he crossed to the opposite wall. Again he climbed and searched for spaces, peering, tapping and levelling off boxes with the palm of his hand. This anxious search had changed his appearance. For the moment confidence had gone. At last he hurried to the room at the back and came out again with a card on a string. 'Closed!' he shouted as he reached the door and threw it open. The room, as if sealed for decades, burst open with noise. A long vehicle was going slowly past with a deck of cars, rattling and straining in their chains, in front was a lorry-load of beer barrels and behind three motor cyclists had come to a shattering halt at the lights. This sudden racket swallowed up any sound that might be made by the one late customer of the shoe shop as he brushed past Thomas in the doorway.

Thomas didn't wait to see more. He hung up the sign inside, then went quickly back to the small room and drew the curtains. Tonight he was conscious that this dingy place with its bulb bowls and cake-tins had an almost homely atmosphere compared with the outer room. It had the dusty smell of safety. He reminded himself – and why should he need to? – that like everyone else he had ties he could break and renew, a home from which he could escape and return. But he was formidably tired. He sat on. It was after six when he finally left the place and locked the shop behind him for the night.

Ten days later he was inclined to laugh that he should be put out in the smallest degree by any customer, let alone one who had never bought shoes. Since then a crowd of people had passed through his hands. Some had been every bit as demanding as the young man. All of them had talked more. There were restless ones amongst them. It was not uncommon to hear how they too had walked and searched and longed for something or other, if not shoes then some other article – or a room, a job, a person. There was nothing strange about this endless search, though it was true each story started in much the same way, with feet. But the discomforts of feet quickly led to discomforts of the heart – how someone had walked in shoes grown savagely tight, from street to street, directed by inquisitive landladies, looking for the friend or lover who had left no scrap or hint of an address. One young man complained bitterly of his cheap shoes with their uneven heels. He had fallen down and slid on his bottom in a dance. Made to feel as clumsy as hell in front of someone who hated . . . who couldn't stand the idea of anyone . . .

'I see,' Thomas had said, '. . . anyone who's not absolutely sure on his feet . . . not footloose.' Yet 'footloose' missed the mark. He was uneasy as soon as it was out of his mouth, remembering how and when the word had been last spoken, on a day he'd taken great pains to forget. He listened to all these stories, long and short. Yet why, he asked himself, give an ear to one young man and not to another?

'Some people,' he said to Mrs Kirk as they locked up after a busy day, 'are never, never satisfied. I can understand that. I can cope with it. What I can't take are the desperate ones.'

'Desperate?' she replied. 'Well I can't say I come across many like that. We've had the violent ones, of course. Don't let them get a foot in the door if you can help it. Once they've a foot in they'll be back and back. They see your comings and goings. They know when you're alone. But desperate, – no I can't say it would bother me too much.' She paused and thought about it. 'You think I'm hard?'

'No – very sensible,' said Thomas.

She accepted this compliment without enthusiasm. 'Anyway,' she said briskly as she went out, 'Miss Borthwick won't find much to complain about when she gets back. Everything's gone smoothly, very smoothly indeed.'

'Has everything gone smoothly, Julia?' Thomas asked as she came downstairs.

'Oh yes, like a swim round a whirlpool!' But some sympathy went with this. Miss Borthwick might or might not come back with peace of mind, but she knew it was something this young man had lost. Whether he had in fact ever had it she couldn't tell. It was not in him now.

September was nearly over. Within two or three days people had changed from cotton into wool and back to cotton again. Still in summer sandals, they brooded over fleece-lined boots. Yet suddenly the sun, hotter than ever, would come back to ripen more fruit on the allotments and lift the battered heads of chrysanthemums from garden fences. In a day or two it was the wind again, an early darkness and floods of rain. Thomas's restlessness came back with a vengeance. His moods changed. On good days distance meant nothing. The ends of the earth could be reached. He had only to take the plunge. He would then become so tired, imagining himself where he was not, that sometimes he had to leave the outer shop and go back for a few minutes to the room behind the curtains. There he would sit taking great breaths of the stuffy air, his head spinning. But on dark days, silent and inturned, he looked at distances inside himself far more disturbing, more alien, than a mere traveller's view. 'Never mind,' said Julia who sensed a change in him. 'No doubt you'll be leaving us soon. Moving on as you'd always meant to. Lucky you have the chance.'

'It's not so easy – not as easy as you think,' said Thomas who had grown silent in the last days.

'Brooding,' said Mrs Kirk to Julia, 'because he's had no holiday. But what does he expect? He made it clear he wouldn't stay. He needs the break of course. You've only to look at him compared to one month back. He has rather a wintry face.'

On Tuesday – the last of the month and two days before
Miss Borthwick was due to return – it was already dark at
three-thirty. The lights went on in the shop. At four when it
brightened they were put off, and went on again at five. The
streets were already lit and in the west the black spires and
chimneys lay against a gash in the sky which was rapidly
closing to one slit of brilliant light.

'I smell water,' said a late customer downstairs as watched
by his wife he bent to lace his shoes. 'There'll be a downpour
before night.' He was a keen fisher, he told Thomas. He
knew something about weather.

'Do you ever think, in your job, of all the sayings connected with feet?' he said as he stood up to test the shoes.

'Putting one's foot in it,' said his wife.

'Standing on one's own feet. Having both feet on the
ground,' said the fisherman. 'That's the one for me when I'm
up to my thighs in the current with a whacking great fish on
the line . . .'

'Oh, these great fish . . .' murmured his wife.

'And you—' said the man with a shrewd glance at Thomas.
'It's not your favourite, I daresay. Not those two feet firmly
planted . . .'

'Why should it be?' said his wife. 'Too young for that.'

'What's age to do with it? It's a matter of common sense,
of not being swayed.'

'He has lots of time.'

'Has he? You mean not like me with my one foot in the
grave. No, no, these aren't comfortable I'm afraid.'

'They're soft,' said Thomas. 'Your foot could work into
them.'

But the man was not the sort to be budged no matter
what currents flowed around. They were the last to leave
from the men's department. Three women came down from
the upper floor with their shoes in green and white carrier
bags and one child in new, red sandals whose eyes never
left her feet as she went down. Mrs Kirk would now be
clearing the long room above. At the far end Julia would be
looking over the day's accounts. It was their turn to lock up.

The gap in the day came at five-fifteen. Thomas went softly round the walls putting in boxes here and there, and very quietly, as if not to disturb the unexpected calm, lifted the stools and chairs into place. It was so quiet that at twenty-five past Mrs Kirk came down a few stairs and looked over the banister.

'Why, Thomas, for a moment I thought you were away!' she exclaimed.

'Not yet,' said Thomas.

'It's very nearly the half-hour.'

'Soon,' said Thomas. 'Don't hurry me, I've still got things to do.'

'I'm *not* hurrying you, Thomas. Just reminding you of the time.' She disappeared up the few stairs.

Thomas went through to the room at the back. This evening he prepared for his departure with particular care. He washed his hands with the new piece of lemon soap which Miss Borthwick kept for her own use and dried them on a clean towel which he found in the table drawer. As he combed his hair he examined himself critically in the mirror. He expected to look tired, but tonight he saw it had gone further than that. This was bone-tiredness. This was the kind that scarred the face and laid a purple shadow in the socket of the eye. Thomas took his jacket from its hook, but before putting it on he sat down and reached for the first book on the pile beside him. Years ago someone had swotted up South America and further on – though less industriously – the Atom, for the Encyclopaedia opened easily on both sections. He turned in a desultory way from the one to the other, reading a sentence or two from each. A page on the Amazon had been well thumbed. In spite of tiredness his interest quickened. Back came the restless search for new ground. From the great river he ran through a spinning universe of electrons, extricated himself, and turned back again to steer down-river amongst rimmed, polished leaves as large as floating platforms. There was no sound but a regular drip, drip of water falling from dense curtains of trees and plants which shut out the sun on either side.

Thomas raised his head and stared straight through the
slit in the curtains, through the shop, and out between a
couple of window posters claiming: 'New styles in Freedom
and Comfort.' Outside on the pavement, his head bisected by
a poster, stood a customer. The half-face, touching the glass,
stared in at him. Thomas moved back an inch. He held the
book in his hands, still with his head bent absorbedly over
it. But his hearing had sharpened dramatically. His room
was not silent. It held his breathing and his heartbeat. It had
a ticking watch and a dripping tap, and once, from the
shelves overhead, came the light, familiar snapping of old
wood fractured by decades of traffic. He heard the bell of
the opening door and he heard the door pressed shut. There
was a pause, and then a soft tread through the shop. The
curtains parted.

The young man stood quietly looking down. There was no
change in his outward appearance. He wore the brown jacket
and the blue shirt, still open-necked in spite of colder days.
The wind had not touched his hair for it was still in its smooth
cone on top of his head. Yet in other ways he was greatly
changed. There was no hint of the man who'd kicked up
havoc amongst shoes. He showed no sign of impatience but
stood smiling, holding the folds of cloth behind him with
both hands like a confident actor appearing before the curtain long after it has gone down. His steady eyes held
Thomas. If need be he could wait forever.

'Oh – you are not after *shoes*!' murmured Thomas, leaning back.

'Company,' said the other softly. 'Company in my search!'

'What search?' said Thomas, raising an arm across his
face. 'What do you want?'

'A foothold,' replied the young man, letting go of the curtain and stepping inside. 'A life for a life cut short. I am
looking for it. For lost years. A foothold is all I ask. And
company – company in my search!'

Thomas sprang through the curtains with a loud cry and
ran through the shop. There was the sound of a stool going
over, a rustling of paper, and one minute later the two

women had run the full length of the floor above and were down the stairs on one another's heels. Thomas lay at the bottom on his side, one arm across his eyes, the other laid on the wall with the hand outspread. Mrs Kirk, detaching this hand, found it cold. There was a small draught coming from behind and she took off her outdoor coat and put it over him. All they could see of his face were the pale, tight lips stubbornly set against all the calling and coaxing in the world. Yet as the girl ran to the phone he suddenly raised his head.

'Oh, Thomas – for a moment I thought you were away!' cried Mrs Kirk for the second time in an hour.

'Not yet,' said Thomas. 'Don't hurry me.'

'Don't joke about it, Thomas!'

'Soon. But not yet,' said Thomas. 'Don't hurry me.'

Five minutes later, refusing all help from Mrs Kirk and Julia, he stood up on his feet. Their advice was not welcome and his indifference alarmed them. They had almost ceased to exist. Mrs Kirk doubted whether he remembered the dragged curtain or the upset stool. For him, her coat lying below the stairs might have been any other old rug. They watched silently as he walked to the door and opened it. But from the threshold he looked back. 'NOT YET, NOT YET!' shouted Thomas through the shop. 'I HAVE STILL GOT THINGS TO DO!'

Gaping at this sudden harangue, the women watched him step out on to the pavement and stagger as the wind caught him. For a moment they waited in the doorway before locking up, then discreetly, at some distance, followed on down the street.

For a while the lights of cars, stopping and starting, swept the empty room. White boxes on the ends of shelves were spotted, a foot-mirror flashed, and from time to time the headlamps of a late lorry would slowly circle the room from floor to ceiling with a bold, yellow glare. But gradually as the night went on fewer and fewer cars passed the windows of the shop. Between three o'clock and five there were none, and no pedestrian went by. The wind died down. The litter of the streets settled again, and there was a total silence on the pavements. Yet here and there on the floor of the shoe shop small scraps of blue and white tissue paper were uneasily stirring, caught in the thin, persistent draught from the back.

A KIND OF POSSESSION

This is a story for those friends of mine who think me modest and tell me that I might have made more of my talents if I had made more of myself. It may be true that I could have gone further if I had asserted myself more strongly. But it is not modesty which has disabled me. There is another and darker reason for my limping way in the world. I cannot emphatically assert myself because I have never since boyhood – since the events related in this story – been fully and constantly certain that I have a whole and inviolable self to assert.

Any story which concerns a hero and a ghost is likely to be regarded as doubly unfashionable and infinitely incredible. But some of the facts can be verified. If you look up the local newspaper files you may read for yourself the report of the accidental death of George Cameron, M.M., in Victoria Street, Edinburgh, on the night of December 31, 1932. The headline is 'Hogmanay Fatality'.

I first met Dod Cameron on a cold wet night in the early winter of 1932. After my evening meal I had gone by tram-car to Bruntsfield to visit a schoolfriend. There was no answer when I rang his door-bell, or when I rattled the flap of his letter-box, or when in exasperation I started hammering the door itself with my clenched fist. I was there by invitation, at the appointed time, and I kept on making my presence heard until a neighbour came out on the landing and told me in a genteel voice that I was wasting my time, that the Johnstons had all gone to a concert in the church hall, and that other folk in the stair were trying to get a bit of peace at their own firesides.

There had been more than one disappointment for me around that time, and more than one cause for indignation.

I had reached a stage in my growing up when I was becoming more aware of myself, more defensive of my pride in being a separate person, and I was always ready to take hurt when I was slighted. I went down the road to Tollcross speaking my mind in a genteel voice to the old woman on the landing and in a plain Scots voice to Watty Johnston. He had forfeited all claims to friendship, going off to a church concert after inviting me up to see a photograph of a Chinese execution which one of his uncles had sent from Canton.

I could not go straight home and admit what had happened. At that time of my life it was easier for me to lie than to tell any truth that humbled me. So I decided to kill time by walking instead of taking the tramcar and, maybe still reacting against the old woman's pan-loaf voice, to turn off the main road and cut across the Old Town. There was nothing genteel about it in those days. It was dirty territory, with a sour smell of poverty in the air. And it was historic territory, loud with the rough old Lowland tongue that was belted out of us at school.

I struck up the High Riggs to the West Port and wound my way down to the Grassmarket. Although the winter darkness had already settled in and a cold wind was blowing up from the Firth of Forth, the streets were still lively. Ragged children played under the gas lamps and in front of yellow-lighted shop windows. Women went about with shawls over their heads, gossiped at the mouths of closes, shouted from tenement windows, waited outside pubs. Old men eddied on corners, muttering and laughing secretly among themselves. Horse-drawn carts clattered over the granite setts, with boys scurrying in pursuit or dangling from the tailboards. A one-armed beggar was singing 'Tipperary'. And high over all rose the Castle, even darker than the night sky behind it.

When the rain started, suddenly pouring down through the smoke without a drizzle of warning, I ran to the nearest close for shelter. It was already crowded with children, who turned on me, jeering at my school uniform, and I fled across the Grassmarket and up the West Bow into Victoria Street, where I found a dry corner for myself in the doorway of a rope-dealer's shop.

It was standing there that I first saw Dod Cameron. The torrent of rain had cleared the whole steep turn of Victoria Street and the West Bow of people and was sluicing it clear of dirt too, tumbling down the gutters like a hill burn and frothing over the choked sivers. I was listening to it, the resounding rattle of its impact on stone and the rumble and rush of its scouring course down the hill, when I heard him shouting from below. He came into sight, a wet scarecrow of a man charging up the middle of the street, his eyes and mouth gaping with terror. 'Come away, Five, up! Keep them going, Tam!' He tore past me, his face lifted towards the top of the rise, where Victoria Street meets George IV Bridge. Just before he reached the top, he jerked his head round to look back over his left shoulder. 'Tam!' he shouted, 'Tam!' He stumbled to a halt, staring down the hill in my direction. I shrank back into the doorway, cold with fear, and watched him standing there in the driving rain and then, bowed and silent, shuffling across to the pavement, where he fell on his knees and wept as I had never seen a man weep before.

I did not hear the door of the rope shop open, but I became aware of the shopkeeper at my back, smoking a pipe and breathing heavily.

'Jist bide here a while, son, till he comes tae himsel'.'

'What's wrong with him?' I asked.

'There's no' much wrang wi' Dod Cameron.' The shopkeeper laid a hand on my shoulder and squeezed some of the chill out of me. 'He's no' daft, jist a wee thing shell-shocked.'

'He looks daft.'

'He's no' himsel' the night.'

'Is he drunk?'

'Like enough. But there's mair in him than drink.'

'You mean the shell-shock?'

The rope-dealer drew on his pipe. 'That man up there,'

he said, wheezily but respectfully, 'won a medal in the war.'

I stared up at the man on the hill, trying to see the hero in the crumpled scarecrow who was dragging himself across the pavement to sit on a doorstep.

'Military Medal,' said the shopkeeper as if he sensed my disbelief, 'and a pension big enough tae feed a dug.'

The storm was passing over and the street was quieter and darker. The thunderous drumming and pouring of rain on granite setts and down narrow gutters had given way to a thin spitting and gurgling, and the reflections of street lamps, no longer shattered into dancing particles, made yellow puddles that threw everything else into deeper shadow.

'Ye're chitterin' cauld, laddie,' said the shopkeeper. 'Awa' hame wi' ye, and gi'e this tae Dod in the passin'.' He held out a shilling. 'Tell him it's his dues frae Robert Wilson. For helpin' me sweep the shop.' He slapped my back. 'On ye go, man. He'll no' bite ye.'

I went out into the thin rain and walked slowly up Victoria Street till I came to Dod Cameron. 'It's from Mr Robert Wilson,' I said, giving him the shilling. 'It's your dues for sweeping.'

Dod looked up at me as he took the coin. I could not see the whole of his face clearly, but I could see his eyes. They were empty of all expression. They were the emptiest eyes I had ever seen. They were like holes that I might fall into.

When I began to boast about him I was a little put out to find that some of my friends had already heard of him. Watty Johnston, of course, declared that his father had told him all about the daft soldier who tried to start the war again every time he was drunk.

'He's not daft,' I said. 'He's shell-shocked.'

'What's the difference?'

'There's a big difference,' I said threateningly.

I was ready to defend Dod against all comers, to explain and justify him to the world. He was a genuine hero, with a medal to prove it. He was a friend of Robert Wilson, one of the shopkeepers in Victoria Street, whom he sometimes helped with the sweeping. He had to do jobs like that because his pension was only enough to feed a dog.

'What kind of dog?' asked Watty.

'Any kind.'

'You mean you didn't see it?' Watty sneered.

I had to defend Dod. I was in the time of life when I needed to mark out a place for myself, and most of us do that by surrounding ourselves with things we can call our own. Dod I could call mine, because I was the only one of my group who had seen him and spoken to him, but I had to make the others set some value on him before the closeness I claimed with him could bring me any credit.

Watty had a way of besting me in matters of this kind, of getting hold of photographs of Chinese executions or getting to meet real people who might have come out of books. He had a way of forcing me to exaggerate my claims, to invent importances for myself, so that I could keep my place and not be crowded out of a separate existence. It was my own fault that he kept jostling me on the subject of Dod. I made so much of my thin knowledge of the shell-shocked soldier that Watty was bound to challenge and deride it. I might have escaped by shifting the ground of our rivalry to some other subject, but one morning Watty presented me not only with another challenge but also with what seemed to be a way of strengthening my position against all his assaults on Dod and myself. His father had told him that the daft soldier did not have to sweep shops to make a living, that he had quite a good pension, considering he was only a young private in the war, and that he had a job in a brewer's stable in the Cowgate.

The next Saturday afternoon, I came across Dod in the Cowgate before I had found any stables. He was sitting at ease on the pavement, with his back against a high stone wall, in a patch of winter sunshine. I came upon him so suddenly that I did not know what to say. He kept his head down but, as I stood there looking at him, he began to twitch nervously. 'Horses,' he said. 'You'll be wanting to see the horses?'

'I came to see you, Mr Cameron,' I answered, with a directness that surprised me almost as much as it startled him.

There was a splendid strangeness about him for a moment, as he glanced at me with those empty eyes of his. They were not any particular colour, his eyes, and their lightness was exaggerated by the redness of his tough-skinned narrow face. But then he sniggered and jerked his head about in a daft way that made me feel ashamed for him. 'Aye, aye,' he said, rising clumsily to his feet, 'everybody wants to see the horses.'

He led me into a shadowed stable where Clydesdales stood in stalls, and he told me their names and made me clap a mountainous rump or two. He seemed to be completely at ease again as he went among them, speaking to them, running his hand over their sleek hides, lifting a huge hoof to examine a new shoe, adjusting a tether. He gave me a locust bean to eat and, chewing its sweet leathery flesh, I followed him in contented silence. The warmth and the smell of that stable come back to me as I write, and the sound of his soft Highland voice and of the shuffling of straw and the snorting and stamping of the great draughthorses, and the sense of refuge. I sat with him at the end of the stable until, after talking for a while about harness, he suddenly fell asleep. Then, taking care not to disturb him, I rose and went happily home.

It was all so easy that first time. The constraint that I might have left then, a self-conscious boy of twelve thrusting himself on a stranger, took its grip of me on my second visit, a week later. I caught Dod unawares outside the stable and he turned away from me, jerking and twitching. We stood apart in awkward silence, looking at different patches of dung-flecked cobbles, until at last he was able to say, 'You're a great boy for the horses.' I followed him into the stable again, but it no longer felt like a refuge. Even the horses seemed to sense our uneasiness, clumping their hooves,

twitching their flanks, tossing their heads and nickering. I
did not stay long, and when I left I thought that I would
never return. But I could not leave him alone. His emptiness
drew me back, and I took to hanging around the Cowgate
in the hope of catching glimpses of him from a distance.

It was Robert Wilson who helped me break this constraint. I was staring into his shop-window one day, debat-
ing with myself whether I should go down to the Cowgate
again, when he came to the door, smoking his pipe and
breathing in that deliberate way of his which made him
seem to be working himself, like a pump of some kind or a
pair of bellows.

'Hemp, that is,' he said, rapping his knuckles against the
side window. Out of politeness I looked at the coil of rope
he had drawn to my attention. 'Manila hemp,' he said. 'They
hang men wi' rope like that.' I took a closer look at the coil,
and he gave a wheezy laugh. 'That's cheered ye up.'

He was an easy man to talk to, although he was as old
as my father, and I found myself reminding him that I had
stood in the doorway with him and watched Dod charge up
the street in the rain, and asking him if he would tell me
what Dod had done to win his medal. I was in such a hurry
to get it all out that the effort left me breathless, and Wilson
laughed again and led me into his shop, breathing heavily
enough to fill us both with air.

He had learned the story of Dod's heroism from a man
who used to live in Candlemaker Row on the other side of
the Grassmarket, a man who had served in the same Highland battalion as Dod. It was a story he plainly enjoyed
telling.

The Germans were in strong positions on the face of a
hill and in the shattered wood on the crest, and for an hour
or two before dusk the British artillery prepared the way for
a night attack by shelling the hill to break up the barbed
wire and empty the trenches and machine-gun emplace-
ments. But, long as the barrage was, it did not seriously
weaken the enemy defences in the wood. When the Highland
battalion that made the first assault started to move for-

ward in torrential rain, they came under heavy machine-gun
fire, and the corporal of Section Five fell while some of his
men were still scrambling out of their water-logged trench.
It was then, when the hesitation of one section might have
slackened the impetus of the whole attack, that Dod won
his medal. Although he was little more than a boy at the
time, he ran forward and took his corporal's place. As he led
the section up the hill, another barrage started. The shells
were meant for the wood on the crest, where the German
machine-guns were still blazing away, but they fell among
the Highlanders on the face of the hill, and Dod was the
only man in Section Five who was later carried out alive,
with a medal waiting for him and some of his wits left behind.

I could see it all, could hear Dod shouting: 'Come away,
Five! Keep them going, Tam!'

Robert Wilson was able to tell me about Tam too. 'Tam
Ogilvy, an aulder man than Dod, near auld enough tae be
his faither. He was a coorse Fifer wi' a voice like a foghorn,
but he was aye thick wi' Dod.'

'Was he killed too?'

'They were a' killed, except Dod. And it micht ha'e been
better for Dod if he had been killed as weel. He's never
gotten very faur frae that hill.'

Dod with his eyes and mouth wide, shouting his heart
out as he ran, until he was running alone.

'When he gets himsel' soakit inside and oot, he aye seeks
back there. He minds Tam Ogilvy and his like better than he
minds the likes o' us.'

Dod running with ghosts that he knew better than any
living men.

'Has he no friends now?'

'Aye,' said Wilson, rising to his feet, lifting himself back
into the dusty world of rope, 'there's you an' me.'

I went straight down to the stable and, without faltering
for a moment, walked in and met Dod again. Maybe because I was so sure of myself, Dod accepted me without a
tremor, and from then till Hogmanay I visited him regularly.

It was a strange companionship, but a true one, for I stopped boasting about him to Watty Johnston and the others and tried to stand between him and the friendless world he had been left in when Tam Ogilvy and the rest of Section Five had fallen on that hill in France. I doubt whether I understood him any better than I understood the Clydesdales, champing and blowing in their stalls, but he was not daft. He could talk when the mood was on him, and he knew about other things besides horses.

We were comfortable together, going about the work of the stable or lying in the loft talking. The only occasions on which that comfort was disturbed were those on which I tried to see too far into him. As we grew into each other's ways, he would sometimes talk briefly about himself, giving me glimpses of his boyhood and once or twice of his training as a soldier, but I had to let him come out with those recollections by himself. If I tried to tap his memory with questions, if I even looked at him too long or too intently, he would jerk his head and shy away from my curiosity. It was as if he could live at peace only so long as he was not made too keenly aware of himself by the thrusting of someone else's attention upon him. Even now I cannot explain him any better than that, and at the time all I knew was that he needed to be sheltered and protected.

Most of the other men who came about the stable – draymen and the like – were unchancy fellows, with knowing eyes and loud mouths. They could be decent enough to Dod when they liked, shouting at him with the same rough kindness that they always showed to me and letting him evade them with an answering smile or quiet word spoken to the horses rather than to them. But there were times when one or other of them would not be cheated in this way and would try to startle him into fuller acknowledgment. I remember a big fellow taking hold of him and shaking him and shouting: 'Answer me! Answer me, ye Hieland gowk!' He gripped Dod's hair, tugged his head back and glared into his eyes. Then, letting him go and turning away from him, he muttered shakily to the others. 'There's naebody there.'

I discovered that it was the draymen who also sometimes filled him full of drink and memory and sent him back to that hill in France. They were good enough men in their way, but there was something in Dod's emptiness that occasionally moved them to cruelty. 'The war's started again, Dod,' I heard one of them shout when they were unyoking one night. 'We'll awa' up tae Johnny Wauchope's for a dram afore ye gang back tae the fechtin'.' It was a night of heavy cloud that might end in rain, and I tugged at Dod's sleeve and asked him to stay with me. He sniggered in that witless way that always made me feel ashamed for him, and he kept sniggering while other draymen, their faces uglier than they usually were, joined in urging him to meet them in Johnny Wauchope's as soon as he had seen to the horses. But I stayed late at the stable, and he did not leave me. When I went home in the rain, I felt more like a man than a boy.

It was different at Hogmanay. They started him drinking in the middle of the day and, when he climbed to the loft where I was waiting for him, he was talking to himself and straddle-legged. He did not seem to notice me, sitting under the skylight with a comic on my knee. He made straight for his camp-bed, took off his jacket and then, suddenly and violently, spewed down his shirt-front. I was on the point of bolting, when he called out to me to fetch up a pail of water.

By the time I had struggled up the ladder with the pail he had stripped himself to the waist. From a distance I watched him wash himself and then the floor beside his bed. He was drawn in the face but sober again, sober and silent. He went for the next pailful of water himself and put his shirt into it to soak. Without looking at me, he came over beside me to get a clean shirt from his chest. Inside the chest, on a shelf holding several small articles, lay a medal.

'Is that your medal?' I asked, still a little nervous of him.

He kept turned away from me, maybe a little ashamed of himself, and told me that I could have it if I wanted it. But it was not said in his usual friendly way, and I was sure that he was just trying to make amends for his drunkenness and vomiting.

'It wasn't me that won it,' I mumbled, my pride helping me to overcome my uncertainty of him in his unfamiliar state.

He had pulled on his shirt and was buttoning it with clumsy fingers. 'Maybe it wasn't me either,' he answered, still keeping me at a distance with his sidelong manner and his huffily defensive tone.

He retreated to his bed and lay down on his side, with his back towards me, and I stared across at him, bewildered by what he had said. I waited there for a long time, until I thought I heard him trying to say something and went over to him. There was a catch in his breathing and, although I could not see his face, I knew that he was desperately unhappy. 'What's wrong?' I asked and, in sudden pity, laid my hand on his shoulder. He did not jerk away from me. After a while he reached round and covered my hand with his.

'You shouldn't be bothering with me, Jamie,' he said, his voice narrow with grief.

I did not know what to do or say, and it may have been my own silence that drew the words from him.

'Nothing in me,' he said. 'Never was, when it came to the bit.'

'But the medal?'

'That's what I mean.'

My own voice was altered too now, hard in my throat as I reluctantly asked, 'You mean you didn't lead Section Five up the hill?'

He squeezed my hand painfully. 'I was in front all right, Jamie,' he assured me, 'but it was Tam that kept us going, Tam Ogilvy . . . that great roaring voice of his, roaring at the lads, roaring at me.'

I was both astonished and ready to believe. It was suddenly easier to understand what had happened, to hear Tam Ogilvy, the coarse Fifer with the foghorn voice, roaring heart into Dod as he ran. I could see Dod running while that great roaring filled him, running until the roaring stop-

ped and he found himself alone and empty. I could understand him and, as I looked down on the back of his head, I
felt myself growing away from him. I could not have explained my feeling then, but now I know that, having reached inside Dod at last, I had out-reached the limits of our
strange friendship. He would never again have been able to
speak to me as he spoke to horses, or to draw me towards
him with those evasive and empty eyes of his. The mystery
had gone out of him, and my pity had become a little
patronizing. There may have been some cruelty in me too.
There was certainly some dim sense of guilt. The consciousness of knowing him at last and, at the same time, of having
in some way lost him made me wait with him until he had
relinquished my hand and settled down to sleep, and made
me promise that I would come back in the evening with a
handsel for his New Year.

There was a smirr of rain in the air that evening, but the
wetness on the streets reflected the lights from windows and
traffic and made the town seem all the gayer for Hogmanay.
Although it was still too early for crowds to be gathering,
there was already an atmosphere of festival, an occasional
drunk man singing his way out of the Old Year. It was the
last day of 1932 and the last day of my childhood.

With a packet of shortbread in my coat pocket for Dod, I
ran part of the way to the Cowgate. As I ran, with my face
held up to the mist and my ears filled with the clatter and
rumble of traffic, I imagined that I was springing forward
to take the corporal's place, leading the section up the dark
hill in a confusion of exultation and terror, hearing Tam
Ogilvy roar courage into me. Running like a mad thing, I
could imagine that roaring swelling inside me, and I knew
how hollow Dod must have felt when the roaring stopped,
when he turned and saw that Tam had fallen. I came to a
halt as he had come to a halt, and I wondered how long he
had waited before the shell burst and blew some of his wits
away and left him lost on that hill for the rest of his life.

The stable was locked and, as I beat my fist on the door,

an old watchman came out of a shed and shouted, 'Get the hell oot o' here!'

'I've got something for Dod Cameron.'

The old man limped across the yard with a hurricane lamp in his hand. 'It's yersel', young Jamie. Ye'll no' see Dod the nicht,' he said sadly.

'Have they taken him to the pub again?'

'Jist that, son. They've ta'en him up till Johnny Wauchope's.'

I had some job finding Johnny Wauchope's. It was at the top of the Cowgate, not far from the stable, but after a glance at its name – the Crown – I trotted past it and into the Grassmarket. There were more people about there, some of the men already grand with drink and trailing retinues of begging children after them. I had a mind to seek help, for the rain was setting in, but two or three boys suddenly swung away from their companions and made for me, yelling, 'See a len' o' yer coat, Jessie!' I was right along the Grassmarket and climbing towards the West Port before I shook them off. When I ventured back, I took up the search on the other side of the Grassmarket, and somewhere along there I noticed for the first time that on the outside of a public house the publican was named as well as the house.

When I discovered at last that J. Wauchope was the licensee of the Crown, I stood outside his door and, every time it swung open, scanned the interior. Dod was not to be seen, but Robert Wilson was there, looking bigger and redder than he did among his ropes, and when he caught sight of me he came out.

'This is nae place for the likes o' you,' he said sternly.

'I've something for Dod, for his New Year.'

He blew on me and held out his hand, but I was set on putting the shortbread into Dod's own hand.

'He's as fu' as a puggy.'

'Can you not get him to his bed?'

Wilson promised to try, but only if I would go home out of the rain. There was no defying him. I turned away and walked reluctantly up to the Grassmarket.

The sense of guilt returned to me, more sharply than before. At the junction of the Cowgate with Candlemaker Row I stopped and looked back, waiting to see whether Wilson would keep his part of the bargain. I do not know how long I waited there, but it was long enough for me to start feeling sorrier for myself than for Dod. I was soaked and chilled, and as I set off homewards again I took the shortbread from my pocket and ate it for a shivery bite.

Just as I reached the foot of the West Bow, I heard the first shouting and looked back once more. A scatter of men came up from the Cowgate, running towards me. He was out in front, urged on by their cries, 'Get efter them, Dod! Up, the kilties!'

He outran his tormentors, who gave up the chase and reeled around with drunken laughter. He took the rise of the West Bow and, holding to the middle of the road, did not see me on the pavement. His face was set towards the hill, eyes and mouth gaping. 'Up, Five, up,' he shouted. 'Keep them going, Tam!'

Without thinking about it, I started running up the pavement, trying to keep pace with him. But the rain lashed into my face, and I was cumbered with wet clothes and stiff with cold. He kept out in front and had almost reached the top of Victoria Street, where it joins the Bridge, before he showed the first signs of hesitation. Panting after him, I watched him slacken pace and look back over his shoulder for Tam Ogilvy. I do not know whether he saw me on the pavement. But I saw the van turning down from the Bridge into Victoria Street, and I opened my mouth to shout a warning to him.

The words that came out of my mouth did not come out of my mind. The sound that came from my throat was not one that any boy could have made. I was suddenly swollen with something other than myself, something that gave a great roar of defiant courage through me, a roaring that reverberated up the hill.

'Keep on, Dod! We're in ahent ye. Up, up!'

I saw Dod's wet face lift into the lamplight. I saw him

turn to his front and leap forward again with fresh determination. He met the bonnet of the van with an impact that
shuddered through my body. He was flung back and, when
I heard his skull break on granite, I dropped out of the
shattered light and the fury of rain into the dark.

Afterwards, while I was still in hospital, two policemen
came to ask me whether I could identify the man who had
shouted to Mr Cameron just before the accident. I told
them that I had not seen anyone except the drunk men at the
bottom of the hill. The policemen said that they had already
spoken to some of those men, who had all been certain
that the man shouting to Mr Cameron was far ahead of
them. They had also spoken to the van driver and his mate,
both of whom were ready to swear that the man must have
been near the top of the hill, not far behind Mr Cameron.
I told them that, although I myself had not been far behind
Mr Cameron, I had not seen any other man.

What more could I say then? What more can I say now?

WHO'S BEEN SITTING IN MY CAR?

'Who's been sitting in my car?' said Jacobine. She said it in a stern gruff voice, like a bear. In fact Jacobine looked more like Goldilocks with her pale fair hair pulled back from her round forehead. The style betokened haste and worry, the worry of a girl late for school. But it was Jacobine's children who were late, and she was supposed to be driving them.

'Someone's been smoking in my car,' Jacobine added, pointing to the ash-tray crammed with butts.

'Someone's been driving your car, you mean.' It was Gavin, contradictory as usual. 'People don't just sit in cars. They drive them.' He elaborated. 'Someone's been driving my car, said the little bear—'

'People do sit in cars. We're sitting in a car now.' Tessa, because she was twelve months older, could never let that sort of remark from Gavin pass.

'Be quiet, darlings,' said Jacobine automatically. She continued to sit looking at the ash-tray in front of her. It certainly looked quite horrible with all its mess of ash and brown stubs. And there was a sort of violence about the way it had been stuffed: you wondered that the smoker had not bothered to throw at least a few of them out of the window. Instead he had remorselessly gone on pressing them into the little chromium tray, hard, harder, into the stale pyre.

Jacobine did not smoke. Rory, her ex-husband, had been a heavy smoker. And for one moment she supposed that Rory might have used an old key to get into the Mini, and then sat endlessly smoking outside the house . . . It was a mad thought and almost instantly Jacobine recognized it as such. For one thing she had bought the Mini second-hand after the divorce. Since ferrying the children had become her main activity these days, she had spent a little money on making it as convenient as possible. More to the point, Jacobine and Rory were on perfectly good terms.

'Married too young' was the general verdict. Jacobine agreed. She still felt rather too young for marriage, as a matter of fact: in an upside down sort of way, two children seemed to be all she could cope with. She really quite liked Rory's new wife, Fiona, for her evident competence in dealing with the problem of living with him.

It was only that the mucky filled ash-tray had reminded Jacobine of the household details of life with Rory. But if not Rory, who? And why did she feel, on top of disgust, a very strong sensation of physical fear? Jacobine, habitually timid, did not remember feeling fear before in quite such an alarmingly physical manner. Her terrors were generally projections into the future, possible worries concerned with the children. She was suddenly convinced that the smoker had an ugly streak of cruelty in his nature – as well as being of course a potential thief. She had a nasty new image of him sitting there in her car outside her house. Waiting for her. Watching the house. She dismissed it.

'Tessa, Gavin, stay where you are.' Jacobine jumped out of the driver's seat and examined the locks of the car. Untouched, both of them.

'Mummy, we are going to be late,' whined Tessa. That decided Jacobine. Back to the car, key in lock and away. They had reached the corner of Melville Street when the next odd thing happened. The engine died and the little Mini gradually and rather feebly came to a halt.

'No petrol!' shouted Gavin from the back.

'Oh darling, do be quiet,' began Jacobine. Then her eye fell on the gauge. He was right. The Mini was out of petrol. Jacobine felt completely jolted as if she had been hit in the face. It was uncharacteristic of her carefully-ordered existence to run out of petrol as for example to run out of milk for the children's breakfast – a thing which had happened once and still gave Jacobine shivers of self-reproach. In any case, another unpleasantly dawning realization, she had only filled up two days ago . . .

'Someone's definitely been driving this car,' she exclaimed before she could stop herself.

'That's what I said!' crowed Gavin. 'Someone's been driving my car, said the little bear.'

'Oh Mummy, we are going to be awfully late,' pleaded Tessa. 'Miss Hamilton doesn't like us being late. She says Mummies should be more thoughtful.'

The best thing to do was to take them both to school in a taxi and sort out the car's problems later. One way and another, it was lunch time before Jacobine was able to consider the intruding driver again. And then, sturdily, she dismissed the thought. So that, curiously enough, finding the Mini once more empty of petrol and the ash-tray packed with stubs the following morning was even more of a shock. Nor was it possible to escape the sharp eyes of the children, or gloss over the significance of the rapid visit to the petrol station. In any case, Tessa had been agonizing on the subject of lateness due to petrol failure since breakfast.

'I shall go to the police,' said Jacobine firmly. She said it as much to reassure herself as to shut up the children. In fact the visit was more irritating than reassuring. Although Jacobine began her complaint with the statement that she had locked her car, and the lock had not been tampered with, she was left with the strong impression that the police did not believe any part of her story. They did not seem to accept either that the doors had been locked or that the petrol was missing, let alone appreciate the significance of the used ash-tray. All the same, they viewed her tale quite indulgently, and were positively gallant when Jacobine revealed that she lived, as they put it, 'with no man to look after you'.

'Of course you worry about the car, madam, it's natural. I expect your husband did all that when you were married,' said the man behind the broad desk. 'Tell you what, I know where you live, I'll tell the policeman on the beat to keep special watch on it, shall I? Set your mind at rest. That's what we're here for. Prevention is better than cure.'

Jacobine trailed doubtfully out of the station. Prevention

is better than cure. It was this parting homily which gave her the inspiration to park the Mini for the night directly under the street light, which again lay under the children's window. If the police did not altogether believe her, she did not altogether believe them in their kindly promises. Anyway, the light would make their task easier, if they did choose to patrol the tree-shaded square.

That evening Jacobine paid an unusually large number of visits to the children's room after they went to sleep. Each time she looked cautiously out of the window. The Mini, small and green, looked like a prize car at the motor show, in its new spotlight. You could hardly believe it had an engine inside it. It might have been a newly painted dummy. The shock of seeing the Mini gone on her fifth visit of inspection was therefore enormous. At the same time, Jacobine did feel a tiny pang of satisfaction. Now let the police treat her as an hysterical female, she thought, as she dialled 999 with slightly shaking fingers. Her lips trembled too as she dictated the number of the car: 'AST 5690. A bright green Mini. Stolen not more than ten minutes ago. I warned you it might happen.'

'Don't worry, madam, we'll put out a general call for it.' Why did everyone tell her not to worry?

'No, it's my car, not my husband's. I haven't got a husband.'

Jacobine tried to sleep after that, but her mind raced, half in rage at the impudence of the intruder, half in imagined triumph that he would be hauled before her, cigarette hanging from his lips, those tell-tale polluting cigarettes . . . It was the door-bell weaving in and out of these hazy dreams which finally ended them. At first she assumed they were bringing round the thief, even at this time of night.

It was a policeman, a new one from the morning's encounter. But he was alone.

'Mrs Esk? Sorry to call so late. About your stolen Mini—'

'Have you found it? Who took it?'

'Well, that's the point, madam. A green Mini, number

AST 5690, reported stolen twenty minutes ago at Ferry Road police station, is now outside your door.'

Jacobine stared. It was true. The Mini was back.

'He must have known you were looking for him.' She blurted out the remark and then regretted it. Silently, Jacobine in her quilted dressing-gown and slippers, and the policeman in his thick night-black uniform, examined the Mini from every angle. The locks were pristine, and the car itself was locked. They examined the dashboard. It was untouched.

'Perhaps there was some mistake?' suggested the policeman in the gentle tone Jacobine had come to associate with his colleagues. 'You only looked out of the window, you said. In the lamp light, you know . . . Well, I'd better be getting back to the station and report that all is well. You don't want to be arrested for driving your own Mini tomorrow, do you?' He sounded quite paternal.

'Look, he only had time for two cigarettes,' said Jacobine suddenly. At least she had curtailed the nocturnal pleasures of her adversary. On the other hand there was a new and rather horrible development. The car positively *smelt*. It did. She did not like to point that out to the policeman, since he had not mentioned it. Perhaps he was embarrassed. It was a strong, pungent, human smell which had nothing to do with Jacobine or the children or even cigarettes. As Jacobine had envisaged someone cruel and even violent when she first saw the ash-tray, she now conjured up involuntarily someone coarse and even brutal.

Jacobine had not thought much about sex since the end of her marriage. Now she found herself thinking of it, in spite of herself. It was the unmistakable animal smell of sex which overpoweringly filled her nostrils.

The next night she put the children to bed early. Still fully dressed, with a new large torch beside her, she took up her vigil in the lobby next to the front door. A little after eleven o'clock, with apprehension but also with excitement, she heard the noise of an engine running. It was close to the house. It was the peculiar coughing start of her own car.

Without considering what she was doing, Jacobine flung open the front door, ran towards the kerb and shouted: 'Stop it, stop it, stop, thief!' The engine stopped running instantly. It was as though it had been cut short in mid-sentence. She wrenched upon the handle of the passenger door, her fingers trembling so much that she fumbled with the familiar door. It did not open. Even locked against her: her own car! In her passion, Jacobine rapped hard on the window.

Nothing happened. Very slowly, she realized that the driver's seat, and indeed the whole of the tiny car, was empty. In the ash-tray, illuminated by the street-lamp like a detail in a moonlight picture, lay one cigarette, still alight. Jacobine was now suddenly aware of her thumping heart as the anger which had driven her on drained away. For the first time she had no idea what to do. After a pause, during which she stood gazing at the locked Mini and the gradually disintegrating cigarette, she walked back into the house. She picked up the car-keys. Even more slowly, she returned to the car and unlocked it. Deliberately, but very gingerly, she climbed into the front seat and touched the cigarette. Yes, warm. The car smelt fearfully.

'Sweetheart,' said a voice very close in her ear. 'You shouldn't have told the police, you know. You shouldn't have done that. You have to be punished for that, don't you?'

Jacobine felt herself grasped roughly and horribly. What happened next was so unexpected in its outrageous nature that she tried to scream out her revulsion. But at the same time a pair of lips, thick hard rubbery lips, were pressed on to her own. The car was still, to her staring frantic eyes above her muted mouth, palpably empty.

'Oh God, I've been taken,' she thought, as she choked and struggled.

'But you like it, don't you, Sweetheart?' as though she had managed to speak aloud. It was not true.

'I'm going to be sick, I think,' said Jacobine. This time she did manage to say it out loud.

'But you'll come back for more tomorrow night, won't you, Sweetheart,' said the voice. 'And we'll go for a drive together.' She was released. Jacobine fumbled with the door once more and, half retching, fled towards the house.

She did not dare leave it again that night but lay in her bed, trembling and shaking. Even a bath did not help to wash away her body's memories of the assault. The next morning, as soon as the children were at school, Jacobine went to the police station. From the start, the man behind the desk was altogether more wary of her, she thought. He listened to her new story with rather a different expression, no less kind, but somewhat more speculative. At the end, without commenting on Jacobine's nocturnal experience, he asked her abruptly if she had ever seen a doctor since the break-up of her marriage.

'I need the police, not a doctor, for something like this,' said Jacobine desperately. 'I need protection.'

'I'm not quite so sure, Mrs Esk,' said the policeman. 'Now look here why don't you have a word first of all with your G.P.? It's not very pleasant being a woman on your own, is it, and maybe a few pills, a few tranquillizers ...'

When Jacobine left the station, it was with a sinking feeling that he had not believed her at all. The rest of the day she agonized over what to do. Ring Rory? That was ridiculous. But Jacobine had no other figure of authority in her life. A lawyer might help, she thought vaguely, remembering the sweet young man who had helped her over the divorce. Yet even a lawyer would ask for more proof, if the police had proved so sceptical. With dread, Jacobine realized that it was up to her to provide it.

About eleven o'clock that night, therefore, she took up her position in the driver's seat. She was not quite sure what to expect, except that there would be a moment's wait while she settled herself.

'I'm glad you're early, Sweetheart,' said the voice conversationally. 'Because we'll be able to go for a really long drive. We've got so much to talk about, haven't we? The

children, for example. I don't really like your children.
You'll have to get rid of them, you know.'

'Don't you dare touch my children,' gasped Jacobine.

'Oh, rather you than me,' said the voice. 'My methods
aren't as pretty as yours. A car crash on the way to school,
for example, which would leave you uninjured . . .'

Jacobine gave a little sick cry. She envisaged those precious tended bodies . . . the recurring nightmare of mother-
hood.

'I know all about crashes and children, their precious
bodies,' went on the voice. He seemed to read her thoughts,
her ghastly images. 'Poor little mangled things.'

Jacobine could no longer bear it. The smell combined
with terror overwhelmed her. And the police station was so
near. Jumping out of the car, abandoning her persecutor,
she ran along the road in the general direction of the station.
A few minutes later she heard the engine start up. The car
was following her. Her heart banged in her chest. She had
time to think that it was more frightening being pursued by
a car, an empty car, than by anything in the world human
and alive, when she gained the safety of the steps. The car
stopped, neatly, and remained still.

'He's threatening the children now. He says he's going
to kill them,' Jacobine began her story. It seemed that she
had hardly gulped it out before a policewoman was taking
her back – on foot – to her house. The policewoman con-
centrated on the fact that Jacobine had left her children
alone in the house while she went out to the car. Indeed,
although it had not occurred to Jacobine at the time, it was
very much outside her usual character. The car was driven
back by a policeman. It looked very chic and small and harm-
less when it came to rest once more outside her front door.

It was two days later that Rory rang up. In between
Jacobine had not dared to leave the intruder alone in the
car at night in case he carried out his threat against the
children during the day. On Saturday he performed the
same act of possession which had initiated their relationship.

On Sunday he brought up the subject of the children again. First he made Jacobine drive as far as Arthur's Seat, then round through silent Edinburgh. Jacobine was tired when she got back, and the Mini was allowed to park beside her house once more. A policeman noted her sitting there, a smouldering cigarette propped above the dashboard, and he heard her cry out. In answer to his questions, she would only point to the cigarette. She was wearing, he saw, a nightdress under her coat. At the time, the policeman was not quite sure whether Jacobine was crying out in terror or delight.

Actually what had forced that strange hoarse sound out of Jacobine was neither fear nor pleasure. It was, in its weird way, a sort of cry of discovery, a confirmation of a dread, but also bringing relief from the unknown.

She had got to know, perforce, the voice a little better during their long night drive. It was some chance remark of his about the car, some piece of mechanical knowledge, which gave her the clue. Proceeding warily – because the voice could often, but not always, read her thoughts – Jacobine followed up her suspicions. In any case, she preferred talking about the car to listening to the voice on the subject of her children. She tried to shut her mind to his gibes and sometimes quite surprisingly petty digs against Tessa and Gavin. He seemed to be out to belittle the children as well as eliminate them from Jacobine's life.

'Fancy Gavin not being able to read – at seven,' he would say. 'I heard him stumbling over the smallest words the other day. What a baby!' And again: 'Tessa makes an awful fuss about being punctual for one so young, doesn't she? I can just see her when she grows up. A proper little spinster. If she grows up, that is . . .'

Jacobine interrupted this by wondering aloud how she had got such a bargain in the shape of a second-hand Mini which had hardly done a thousand miles.

'Oh yes, Sweetheart,' exclaimed the voice, 'you certainly did get a bargain when you bought this car. All things considered. It had always been very well looked after, I can tell you—'

'Then it was your car,' Jacobine tried to stop her own voice shaking as she burst out with her discovery. 'This was your car once, wasn't it?'

'There was an accident,' replied the voice. He spoke in quite a different tone, she noticed, dully, flatly, nothing like his usual accents which varied from a horrid predatory kind of lustfulness to the near frenzy of his dislike for the children. 'Tell me.'

'It was her children. On the way to school. There was an accident.' It was still quite a different tone, so much so that Jacobine almost thought – it was a ridiculous word to use under the circumstances – that he sounded quite human. The smell in the car lessened and even the grip which he habitually kept on her knee, that odious grip, seemed to become softer, more beseeching than possessing.

'She worked so hard. She always had so many things to do for them. I was just trying to help her, taking them to school for her. It was an accident. A mistake. Otherwise why didn't I save myself? An accident, I tell you. And she won't forgive me. Oh why won't she forgive me? I can't rest till she forgives me.' It was piteous now and Jacobine heard a harsh, racking sobbing, a man's sobbing which hurts the listener. She yielded to some strange new impulse and tentatively put out her hand towards the passenger seat. The next moment she was grasped again, more firmly than before; the assault began again, the smell intensified.

'I've got you now, Sweetheart, haven't I?' said the voice. 'It doesn't matter about her any more. Let her curse me all she likes. We've got each other. Once we get rid of your children, that is. And I'm awfully good at getting rid of children.'

When Rory rang on Monday he was uneasy and embarrassed.

'It's all so unlike Jacobine,' he complained later to Fiona. 'She's really not the type. And you should have heard some of the things she told the policeman this fellow in the car had done to her.'

'Oh those quiet types,' exclaimed Fiona. Without knowing Jacobine intimately, she had always thought it odd that she should have surrendered such an attractive man as Rory, virtually without a struggle. 'Still waters,' Fiona added brightly.

Rory suggested a visit to the doctor. He also wondered whether the strain of running a car ... Jacobine felt the tears coming into her eyes. Why hadn't she thought of that? Get rid of him. Get rid of the car. Free herself.

'Oh, Rory,' she begged. 'Would you take Tessa and Gavin for a few days? I know it's not your time, and I appreciate that Fiona's job—'

'I'll have them at the weekend,' suggested Rory, always as placating as possible, out of guilt that Jacobine, unlike him, had not married again. 'Fiona's got a marketing conference this week and I'll be in Aberdeen.'

'No, please, Rory, today, I implore you. I tell you what, I'll send them round in a taxi. I won't come too. I'll just put them in a taxi this afternoon'

But Rory was adamant. It would have to be the weekend.

That afternoon, picking up Tessa and Gavin from school, Jacobine very nearly hit an old woman on a zebra crossing. She had simply not seen her. She could not understand it. She always slowed down before zebra crossings and yet she had been almost speeding across this one. Both children bumped themselves badly and Gavin in the front seat, who was not wearing his safety belt (another odd factor, since Jacobine could have sworn she fastened it herself), cut himself on the driving mirror.

'That's your warning,' he said that night. 'The children must go. You spend too much time thinking about them and bothering about them. Tiresome little creatures. I'm glad they hurt themselves this afternoon. Cry babies, both of them. Besides, I don't want you having any other calls on your time.'

And Jacobine was wrenched very violently to and fro, shaken like a bag of shopping. The next moment was worse. A cigarette was stubbed, hard, on her wrist, just where the veins ran.

Even at the instant of torture, Jacobine thought:
'Now they'll have to believe me.'

But it seemed that they didn't. In spite of the mark and
in spite of the fact that surely everyone knew Jacobine did
not smoke. A doctor came. And Rory came. Jacobine got
her wish in the sense that Tessa and Gavin were taken away
by Rory. Fiona had to break off half-way through her
marketing conference, although you would never have
guessed it from the cheery way she saluted the children.

'Just because their mother's gone nuts,' Fiona said
sensibly to Rory afterwards, 'it doesn't mean that I can't
give them a jolly good tea. And supper too. I have no idea
what happened about their meals with all that jazzing about
at night, and running around in her nightie, and screaming.'

Then Rory took Jacobine down to a really pleasant
countrified place not far from Edinburgh, recommended by
the doctor. It had to be Rory: there was no one else to do it.
Jacobine was very quiet all the way. Rory wondered whether
it was because he was driving her car – the car. But Fiona
needed the Cortina to fetch the children from school. Once
or twice he almost thought Jacobine was listening to something in her own head. It gave him a creepy feeling. Rory put
on the radio.

'Don't do that,' said Jacobine, quite sharply for her. 'He
doesn't like it.' Rory thought it prudent to say nothing. But
he made a mental note to report back to Fiona when he got
home. For it was Fiona who felt some concern about des-
patching Jacobine in this way.

'It's really rather awful, darling,' she argued, 'taking her
children away from her. They're all she had in her life. Poor
dotty girl.'

'They are my children too,' said Rory humbly. But he
knew just what Fiona meant. He admired her more than
ever for being so resolutely kind-hearted: it was wonderful
how well she got on with both Tessa and Gavin as a result.
Fiona also took her turn visiting Jacobine when Rory was
too busy. There were really no limits to her practical good
nature. And so it was Fiona who brought back the news.

'She wants the car.'

'The car!' cried Rory. 'I should have thought that was the very last thing she should have under the circumstances.'

'Not to drive. She doesn't even want the keys. Just the car. She says she likes the idea of sitting in it. It makes her feel safe to know the car's there and not free to go about wherever it likes. I promise you, those were her very words.'

'What did Dr Mackie say? It seems very rum to me.'

'Oh he seemed quite airy about it. Talked about womb transference – can that be right? – anyway that sort of thing. He said it could stay in the grounds. Like a sort of Wendy house, I suppose. She hasn't been making very good progress. She cries so much, you see. It's pathetic. Poor thing, let her have the car. She has so little,' ended Fiona generously.

So Jacobine got her car back. Dr Mackie had it parked as promised in a secluded corner of the gardens. He was encouraged to find that Jacobine cried much less now. She spent a great deal of time sitting alone in the driver's seat, talking to herself. She was clearly happier.

'It's much better like this,' said the voice. 'I'm glad we got rid of your children the *nice* way. You won't ever see them again, you know.' Jacobine did not answer. She was getting quite practised at pleasing him. He was generally waiting for her when she arrived at the Mini in its shady corner.

'Who's been sitting in my car?' she would say in a mock gruff voice, pointing to the heap of butts in the ash-tray. But in spite of everything Jacobine still looked more like Goldilocks than a bear. Indeed, her face had come to look even younger since she lost the responsibility of the children – or so Fiona told Rory.

Jacobine had to be specially charming on the days when Fiona came down to see her, in case He got into her car and went back to find the children after all. She thought about them all the time. But she no longer cried in front of Him. Because that made Him angry and then He would leave her. She had to keep Him sitting beside her. That way the children would be safe. From Him.

THE HAUNTED CHIMLEY

My acquaintance with Noaker Todd began during a depressed period in the graph of my career, when I had been compelled to recognize that, although my poetry was a much better mousetrap than the models previously available, the world stubbornly refused to beat a pathway to my door, and that the world's pigheadedness was probably incurable.

This is a turning point in any poet's life, and I only wish that more poets would turn at that point. Anyway, I did, and I made the bold decision that I would reject the universe of ideas and become some kind of tycoon, grinding the faces of the masses and stripping assets and all the other things that really stupid people do and get their names in the gossip columns for.

One of the first snags I met was that the Workers' Educational Association didn't run classes in asset-stripping or face-grinding, and I was faced with the job of doing original research, which didn't help much because the public libraries don't go in much for classified sections on these rudimentary disciplines either

The situation was ludicrous, like most situations. I had a divine gift, which I had discarded because it didn't pay the rent, and as a substitute I had an intelligence quotient which if fed back into Boulder Dam would have fused the entire United States in a wanny. But I couldn't get the thing started. Let me put it this way. If somebody had offered me a job as the chairman of an asset-stripping multi-national combine, or the hatchet man of a face-grinding conglomerate, I would have been able to strip and grind like magic. I just couldn't get started. The Labour Exchange didn't seem to have the idea, and their suggestions were a long way from the gossip columns.

I'll get to Noaker Todd in a minute. The situation has to

be given an ambience, a provenance, and I'm in this story too. My problems *matter*.

In the end, or the beginning, I was forced to desperate measures, like lowering my suitcase out of a second-floor window in the toney West End district of Glasgow, strolling downstairs, making a rapid breenge through the close to pick up my worldly goods, and sauntering like one demented to an address in the ancient Townhead vicinity of the city which I had picked up from a postcard in the window of a mean tobacconist's shop in George Street.

It read, 'Furnished room going cheep, and oblidge.' No poet could resist a room that went cheep.

I never actually heard it going cheep, but crises make strange bedfellows, or something of the kind, and I was in no position to choose. When I climbed the two flights in Glebe Street, Townhead, Glasgow, and banged on the door, it opened to reveal a face that a less sensitive man would have kicked at once. But there was something, some je ne sais quoi, in Noaker's expression, that spoke to me. Dishonesty, I think it was.

'Do you have gainful employment, if I can use foul language?' he asked.

'I start on Monday as an inquiry clerk with British Railways,' I parried wittily.

'You're in,' he replied, heaved my suitcase into the darkness behind him and jostled me downstairs to Donnelly's Bar, where he borrowed my last pound and spent it with splendid abandon.

A pound is not a lot, and wasn't a lot even then, but Donnelly's special Icelandic brandy-type varnish works faster than a bullet in the brain, and that night I sank into the routine coma which was to be my way of life in the Toonheid.

It was actually true that I had employment as an inquiry clerk with British Railways. I even went so far as to answer inquiries, sometimes truthfully, and I more importantly became a peripheral part of the Toonheid society which, for me, was dominated by Noaker Todd.

Noaker was a man of little formal education, but he had other gifts, such as futile optimism and a lust for robbing gas-meters, which established him as a genuine human being and often drove me mad. He had not actually been inside for several years at the time I made his acquaintance, but he was always in hopes of pulling off a coup that would make him the criminal of the century and earn him fifty years in solitary, serialized by the *News of the World*.

His career as a master criminal, he felt, had been seriously inhibited by his domestic situation. His endlessly patient wife Emily suffered from a passionate respectability and a compulsion to make chips, and his son Alastair, who was a thoroughgoing boil in the backside, was studying humanities at Glasgow University and believed in the Protestant ethic. Noaker, in fact, was a man beleaguered by forces of his own making, and after a few evenings of his company in Donnelly's Bar, I sometimes thought, Well, Hell mend him.

But he was a man you couldn't dismiss lightly, and I was forced to listen to him one night in Donnelly's Bar when he got on to a philosophic kick.

'It's like this, Jimmy,' he told me earnestly.

'My name is Louis,' I protested.

'Aye, that's right. Well, it's like this, Louis, Jimmy. The theory I've got is, I am wan of these people born oot their time, you know? Maybe I went and slipped through some kinda time warp or other out the seventeenth century to which I rightly belang, see? Or wan day when I was distracted and not screwing the nut proper, somebody beamed me doon into the salubrious vincity of Toonheid with wan of yon shoogly light things they've got in Star Trek. Anyway, I am right out of my time, Jimmy, Louis.'

This ringing declaration was made in Donnelly's on one of those evenings when the conversation is rich and salty, and the minions pussyfooting around serving glasses of Donnelly's special Icelandic brandy-type varnish live a life of pure hell.

Big Ned the barman, who is a deeply unimpressionable citizen, averred that that kind of talk almost goaded him into letting Noaker have one in the teeth for starters. The Noaker threw him a sneering glance that bounced harmlessly off Ned and broke three glasses at the end of the bar.

'See,' the Noaker went on, 'it's obvious to anybody that I am not fittit for the essential squalor of a manky boozing establishment of this kind. The elegant salons of Empire France, and a' that kinna upper-class rubbish, is mair in my line. Or perchance wan of yon Roman baths, wi' a built-in distillery and a vomitorium. High-tone stuff.'

'Aw, nark it, Noaker,' said Charley Crum, the Toonheid Tealeaf, whose fingers were inching towards my drink automatically. 'Whit I mean, we a' recognize your intellectual prowess and that, but you're a born scruff like everybody else.'

'In the first place,' said Noaker, 'kindly remove your mitt from my inside pocket because I've got a poisoned rat-trap in it, and in the second place you would not even have knew the words intellectual prowess if I hadny of coached you for two days in the pronunciation of the phrase, and in the third place belt up and refrain from giving us the boak. I was made for better things. It is only the callous injustice of Fate that has turned me to crime – it's my hysterical response to the horror of destiny.'

'And you are nae use at crime either,' Charley returned brutally. He was spluttering a bit, though, and I noticed my drink had mysteriously been beamed down on to another planet.

'That,' said Noaker, 'is simply explicated by the sheer lack a opportunity. In the name a Heaven, where's the chance a pullin' off a historical cowp of criminal darin' and ingenuity and that, in a dump like Toonheid, which I may add is disappearin' round our ears while we staun here? Where are the irreplaceable collections a Van Gogs and that? You gonny fun a priceless Shakespeare folio planked up a close in Glebe Street, eh?'

'Ach, you could go somewhere else, Noaker, couldn't you? Maybe up a close in Pollokshields or somewhere –

that's where they keep things like Van Gogs. Zat a breed a dug?'

Noaker was fairly blistering with contempt; and with some cause, for Charley, in spite of his nickname, was probably the most incompetent tealeaf in the history of crime. He had a proclivity for stealing things like rusting tram-rails, or concrete tank-traps, which even the most enthusiastic antique-collectors find it difficult to slip through the trade. Stealing other people's drinks was probably the only talent he had developed to commercial level.

'You'd be a great guy to take on a big art raid,' Noaker snarled. 'Tell you to go for the Ming porcelain and you'd come oot wi' an airmful a greyhounds. Lend us a quid and cease your maudlin mutterin's.'

Charley blenched and resisted feebly as Noaker's masterful hands ran over his body and extricated a rolled-up pound note.

'That was for to pey the slater,' Charley protested. 'There's a funny noise in the chimley.'

Noaker broke off in the middle of a coarse retort and that familiar look passed over his ferrety features.

'A noise in the chimley? A ghost?'

'Ach, whoever heard a ghosts in the Toonheid,' Charley cried, his lip trembling at the sight of his pound note vanishing over the bar. 'They couldny scrape a livin' oota this place.'

'If a say it's a ghost, it's a ghost. Listen, this is it. Ah tell ye, ma cerebellum is fair comin' to the bile with plans for wealth bigger than that foreign nyuck Montezuma. Shut up while the wee cogs an' electrical relays an transisitors and that, inside me heid, compute the fraud a the century.'

Charley glumly accepted a noggin of Donnelly's special Icelandic brandy-type varnish and muttered, 'Nae good is gonny come a this.'

I must say I never found it easy to follow the convolute mechanism of the Noaker's mind, and the idea of turning a rattling chimney into a gold-mine was not one that would have occurred to my pedestrian temperament. Still, none of us is Noaker Todd, thank God.

That evening found the Noaker settled in Charley Crum's three-stairs-up but-and-ben, and a quite astonishing collection of other people. When I squashed into the lobby I was met by Charley, looking glum, furtive and criminal, and holding out a syrup tin with a slot gouged in the top.

'Tenpence a skull,' he said. 'Noaker says that's what it takes to cover the overheads and that. It's a non-profit organization.'

'Everything you're connected wi' is a non-profit organization,' Noaker intervened. 'You can get in free this time, Louis,' he added to me. 'I honestly conjecture that this time I have went an' struck your actual pey dirt.

'Now then, ladies and gentlemen, and best of order if you please,' he cried. 'Efter extensive historical research, and even reading three or four books, and tappin' a lotta telephones, I have went and elicited the bazaar information that there was this aristocratic burd in the eighteenth century or some time like that, and she went a bundle on this impoverished student that lived in the Toonheid.'

The mob jammed into the kitchen looked impressed and sceptical at the same time, and one hatchet-faced lady shouted, 'Away and bile your can, Noaker Todd. There was nae such thing as the Toonheid in the eighteenth century.'

'Aw, listen tae that criminal ignorance of Clyde navigation,' Noaker appealed to the customers. 'It's well known that it was the stout warriors of Toonheid that held back the flamin' hordes a Romans when Caesar tried to put the hems on Scotland . . . oh, even further back than the eighteenth century. The fourteenth century, even. Are you tryin' to impung the honour of my native city or something?'

'He's right,' Charley C: m insisted. 'I wance fun a Roman helmet in a back-court just aff the High Street. A polis helmet, I think it was. But it was Roman, right enough. What I mean, it stauns to reason, doesn't it?'

This astonishing piece of illiteracy hushed the crowd momentarily, and by a miraculous intervention, a distinct rap, rap, rap made itself heard from the fireplace.

'It's here!' the Noaker cried. 'The ghost a Lady Arabella McGlumpher!'

'Who the hell is Lady Arabella McGlumpher?' somebody asked. 'She's no' worth tenpence, that's for sure.'

'Help ma boab, does romance mean nothin' to youse flinty-hearted nyucks? Are your minds that shut to ordinary human sympathy that you canny shed wan wee tear for this lassie that was star-crossed in love and flung oot into the street withoot a tosser except for a signet ring and a daud of black pudden her faithful governess had slipped into her bodice while her merciless faither Lord McGlumpher was runnin' roon the hoose turning' her pictures to the wa'?

'Whit I mean to say, visualize the scene, and Charley Crum, you keep your sticky fingers ooty that syrup tin.

'Here is this delicately bred bird, greeting her eyes oot, big dugs snappin' at her heels, and the brutal Lord McGlumpher rakin' through the kitchen drawer for a whip, so's he could do a big production number wallopin' her a' the way doon the Maryhill Road. Does that no' give youse the jandies?'

'Dirty shame,' said somebody, and somebody else said, 'I don't know, it sounds awright. Actually I quite fancy wallopin' a good-lookin' bird doon the Maryhill Road. Were her claes aw torn an' that? They're usually aw torn. Ah fancy that.'

'So,' said the Noaker firmly. 'So, as I was sayin' before you shoved your big perverted gub into the conversation . . . claes aw torn for God's sake – is that aw you think aboot? Squalor and lust and the pleasures of the flesh. You would sicken a pig.'

'You're dampt right,' said the interrupter. 'Ah think aboot it aw the time.'

'Awright, then,' the Noaker said reasonably, 'her claes were aw torn. Okay. But does it no' wring your withers to picture it – and she had to run aw the wey, you know. They hadny run the trams oot to Maryhill in these days. It was murder.'

'Was it snawin'?' asked the pervert.

'Aye, sure, it was blawin' a monsoon if you like. Listen, if you keep embellishin' this heart-rendin' narrative the poor bitch is never gonny get to the Coocaddens, never mind Toonheid.

'So anyway, she kept breengin' doon the road towards her poor but honest lover, who was loafin' aboot outside Donnelly's Bar waitin' for the result of the two-thirty, and – Listen! There she is again!'

And indeed, there she was again, the ghostly rap rap rap. The audience gasped dutifully.

'Don't worry, hen,' said the Noaker. 'You're among friends. So, after ordeals unknown to medical science, Arabella fell into the embrace of her handsome Sanny, who had just knocked off fifty groats on a rank outsider and was ready to walk through a fire for his beloved, as long as it wasny lit. He grasped her exhausted form and swept her up the close in a wanny.'

'That's the game,' shouted the pervert. 'Now we're gettin' to it. Through the back close, in the dunny, and away wi' the goalie!'

'Aw, belt up and wipe the spittle aff your chin,' said the Noaker. 'He tenderly bore her three stairs up and was tending her wounds and slippin' a jolt a cheap wine into her when there was a thunder of hooves up the stair. The vengeance of Lord McGlumpher had caught up wi' them.

'It took five lackeys to over power Sanny, who was wild wi' love and heroism and cheap wine. He was smuggled aboard a hell ship bound for the plantation in Gorbals, and never heard of again.'

'That's fair enough,' said the pervert. 'They eat their young ower in Plantation.'

'Now we get to the denowment and that. Lord McGlumpher's aristocratic lip curled up like a cheap perm, and a lotta froth squirted oot aw ower the table. He was fair bealin' wi' rage.'

' "Must you pursue me to the ends a the earth or somethin'?" cried Arabella.

' "Naw," he snarled, "only to the Toonheid. Your behaviour has blotted the family escutcheon to hell. You are
not fit to live." And, after burstin' a few blood vessels, he
ordered his lackeys to brick her up. They were terrible hot on
brickin' people up in these days – an aristocrat could hardly
leave the hoose withoot a lorry-load of bricks just in case he
took a sudden notion.

'So despite her screams for pity and polite requests to be
given a break for God's sake, they got into it wi' the trowels
at the double and suddenly, there she was, gone! Inside that
very wall!'

Oh, the Noaker had his audience now. Even the pervert
had momentarily stopped brooding about torn clothes and
was staring, rapt, at the fireplace.

A fresh burst of sound rewarded him. A slate clattered
down into the grate followed by a blow-down of soot the
size of a cobalt bomb.

'Swindler, cheat, fraud, rotten get,' and other epithets,
the audience shouted. But the soot was a mercy, in a way,
because as it swirled towards them they fled without waiting to
lynch the Noaker. As the fall-out subsided, I saw the Noaker
and Charley Crum doing their black minstrel routine while
wrestling for the syrup tin. Noaker won, of course.

'Three quid,' he said. 'Three lousy quid.'

'You owe me a quid.'

'Ach, don't deave me wi' your tales of woe, Charley.
Don't you realize my dreams of wealth have evaporated
like condensed milk? I intended to work this twice nightly
and have fortune-tellin' and spiritualism and everythin'. I
tell you, I was born in the wrang century. And no doubt
there'll be a posse of satisfied customers lurkin' at the close-
mooth to administer a kickin' when I emerge. What are you
gapin' at?'

'It's a helluva cauld for June all of a sudden,' said Charley.
His teeth were chattering and so, I discovered, were mine.
'An' another thing, it's months since I made any soup.'

'My God, it's freezin' in here right enough,' Noaker
agreed. 'What the hell has soup got to do wi' it?'

'Well, that's a bloody bone, innit!'

Certainly the object he was pointing at, although it was encased in soot, had all the outward appearances of a bone, though none of us showed any eagerness to examine it more closely. And at that moment there was a distinct sound from the chimney. Rap rap rap. Rap . . . rap . . . rap.

'It's nearly the Morse code for SOS,' the Noaker breathed. With a noise like a pistol shot the mirror above the fireplace broke across the middle.

'My God,' said Noaker. 'The entire story was true. She's in there right enough. It must have been a genuine burst of telephony I was experiencin'. Get everybody back up – we'll charge double.'

'I'm gettin' to hell oota here,' Charley quavered, and the Noaker's shoulders slumped.

'Aye, it's too late. Always too late. I've been hoisted wi' my own canard or somethin'. Oh well, a mad breenge to Donnelly's Bar before the hordes a Tuscany catch up wi' us.'

'What about Lady Arabella?' I queried diffidently.

'Ach, to hell wi' her, she can rot in there while we think up somethin'. Last man in the boozer's a jessie.'

I was glad enough to leave Charley's kitchen, because even after we closed the door behind us, there was an odd noise from inside, a faint whirring and bouncing, as if the room were inhabited by a demented budgie.

As we breenged, I pondered on the malign fate that always waited to louse up the Noaker's grandiose plans. But when I saw him adroitly fending off three enraged customers to reach the safety of the pub without a scratch, I knew that one day, by sheer stupid optimism, he must triumph.

THE CURATOR

Crosbie walked along, his eyes turned to the shop windows, a suitcase in his hand. He went at the pace of the crowd, and the crowd was in no hurry; foreigners, half of them, all of them able to afford a holiday in Britain, and a quick tour of Scotland; all of them able, then, to walk into any of these shops and order the sealskin brooches, the mink, the tartan, the Shetland jumpers, the shortbread and bottles of whisky.

Everything was for the tourist. The restaurants were packed to the door, the pubs let out light and heat and great whiffs of malt and tobacco, and in the bookshops stood brown and yellow men with their faces to the wall and their noses deep in paperbacks. There were too many tourists, too many *young* people. He shifted his suitcase to the other hand, and stared at the strollers to see if there were any of his own generation; but prosperity rejuvenates, on the surface, anyway, and the gentlemen with cameras and casual shorts forged along with an air of youth. White beards showed off the affluent tan, tinted glasses suggested brighter suns and broader horizons; and yet, alien as they were, these were the people he knew, his bread and butter; in a way, the only people he met.

He was curator of the Memorial, a great thrusting edifice which tossed a whirl of turrets to the sky, and commemorated a man who had done some service to the city. Nobody was sure what exactly J. Crawford Melvin had done. A library or two, a park, an art gallery, a lot of civic amenities and architectural horrors were laid to Mr Melvin's credit – but everyone knew his name and memorial.

On duty, George Crosbie wore a uniform which made him look something between a policeman and a bus inspector. He crept about, hunch-shouldered, suspicious, while his assistant beamed and touched his hat as he pocketed tips. Crosbie was never offered so much as a penny.

The two men changed duties on alternate weeks. One week Crosbie was at the entrance, taking the money and pushing pink tickets through the little window. Next week, he would be on one of the platforms, urging the crowds to keep moving. Drooping, long-nosed, he watched the legs shuffle past him, slim hips in jeans, fat Americans, big crimplene-clad bottoms, and lovely young legs in tights and sandals; every back turned, everyone going away from him, up and up the ever narrowing spiral.

A more gregarious man would have enjoyed the constant coming and going, but Crosbie liked his own company. That, and the pigeons. The Memorial harboured whole colonies of them, nesting in carved cornices and dizzy niches where the dust swirled and grey droppings streaked the walls and crusted the stone curlicues.

For some unaccountable reason, Crosbie loved the pigeons – perhaps because his partner disliked them. The genial Mackenzie was not above making capital out of them. He pointed them out to visitors, holding on to nervous, protesting girls who wanted to look but daren't in case they turned dizzy; he encouraged the men with the cameras to snap them from perilous positions; but then, when he had roused his audience to maudlin ecstasies over the glimpse of smooth eggs or little bald heads and gaping beaks, he would dash their enthusiasms with disgust. 'Tchah! Dirty brutes! They smear everything, they foul all the gutters. Stand here on a hot day, and the smell would make you sick!'

But Crosbie, friendless, lacking the gift of easy chat, was somehow drawn to the despised birds. At quiet moments he would peer over the balustrades, checking up on the nests, watching the parents come and go. He didn't want to share the sight with the visitors. He even resented Mackenzie knowing about them. Sometimes, at night, he would imagine he heard them cooing softly, talking as husband and wife talk in bed together, and in the early mornings he heard the first rustle as they stirred themselves to fly into space in search of food. It hurt him a little that when he laid out crusts for them they gobbled the bread so dispassionately.

To them, it was no different from the scraps they picked up on the ground.

Every day, Crosbie swept the 303 steps of the Memorial, from the bottom up. It was his responsibility to keep the place clean, to look after the photographs and documents in the museum room, and to make returns of the tickets issued to visitors. He had an 'office', a bleak little cupboard at the bottom of the stairs where he hung his coat and stored his cleaning materials and sometimes made a cup of tea. Mackenzie was never allowed into this office. All *he* had to do could be done in the cubby-hole where he sold the tickets.

Crosbie had his reasons for not allowing anyone into his office. He was actually living in the Memorial, and had been doing so for some months. Before that, he had had a room, a bleak and grudging room where he slept and kept his clothes. In all the time he had been there, neither he nor the landlady had added one homely touch. He accepted the cheap yellowish linoleum, the draggled pink candlewick, the bits and pieces of carpet. There was never the glow of a fire, but in the worst of winter a paraffin heater oozed fumes from a thin blue flame.

And then, suddenly, the room was wanted for a nephew returning from abroad. He protested. There was nowhere for him to live, nowhere at all – not, at least, until the summer crowds had gone, and then the lodgings they vacated would cost much more than he had been paying up till now. He begged his landlady for more time, and finally he quarrelled with her, so that she ordered him out on the spot. He packed the little he had, took it to work with him, and that night, when he locked up the Memorial, he stayed inside.

Ever since, he had been making it his home. At night he slept on two chairs, covered with his coat and an old travelling rug. He washed and shaved in the 'office', and kept a secret cache of bread and butter and tea. Sometimes he fancied a slice of bacon for breakfast, but he was afraid to cook it in case the smell gave him away; and in the evenings he had to see Mackenzie off the premises, and make a pre-

tence of getting ready to follow him. He could have left with
him, and spent an hour or two in a tearoom or pub; but that
meant re-entering the Memorial, and perhaps being seen;
and anyway, he was best to keep away from pubs. The
Memorial had no lavatory. After one nerve-wracking night
of nipping in and out to the Gents', he had decided that
abstinence had its virtues.

He looked forward to his assistant's day off. It meant that
he could rise at leisure, maybe boil an egg for breakfast, and
leave the washing-up till later. His own day off, on the other
hand, was a burden to him. There was nothing to do but
wander the streets like a tramp, always carrying the suitcase
which held his uniform. 'Off for the weekend?' Mackenzie
asked regularly, nodding at it, and Crosbie, surly, told him
to mind his own business.

It was enough to make anyone surly. The night before,
Mackenzie was given the key. It was a huge heavy key, so
large and obsolete that if he had tried to have a duplicate
made it would have been news. This meant that there was no
chance of nipping back in for a sleep. It meant, too, that
Crosbie had to leave in his uniform, and change at the railway station. Somehow it would have seemed all wrong to
wear uniform off-duty. He had a need to appear anonymous,
undistinguished by any official marks, just as, at the
Memorial, he had no identity beyond that of curator.

He did the thing in comfort, to make it something of an
occasion. He paid for a changing room, had a bath and a
shave, repacked his case, and made the ritual last as long as
possible. This done, he took his dirty clothes to a launder-
ette, and sat gloomily, watching them whirl away through
the sudsy window. Next he went to a pub, had a drink or
two, bought himself a fish supper, and then went to a Working Men's Hotel. Few of the men there had ever worked, and
the word 'hotel' was a euphemism. It was, in fact, a model
lodging house, and every time Crosbie went there he vowed
never to do it again.

The entrance was reasonable enough, broad stone stairs
well scrubbed, going up to the sleeping quarters and down

to the kitchen. There was always a smell of soup coming from the kitchen, but after beer and fish and chips it lost some of its appeal. Beyond the entrance, the rest of the hostel was depressing, the common room with sawdust on the floor, and the television set flickering dimly through the smoke; the derelict men in caps and overcoats which they never seemed to take off; and upstairs, the beds, adequate and clean, in cubicles, but meagre in space, and surrounded all night with a racket of groans and coughing. It was more comfortable than stretching across two chairs in the museum room, but Crosbie always fell asleep feeling shamed and humiliated and desperately homesick for the Memorial.

He was always there early, too early, waiting for Mackenzie to let him in; and Mackenzie seemed, almost spitefully, to wait till the last possible moment. Shivering, Crosbie would wait on one of the seats in the gardens, watching his breath cloud the cold morning. His feet left dark marks on the grey dew, and the wood of the seat felt damp. A few of his pigeons fluttered down, and sparrows gathered round his feet, cheeping loudly, tilting their cheeky brown heads. The great clock, overlooking the gardens, jerked on, a half-minute at a time, and the top pinnacles of the Memorial seemed to recede into a faint mist. Two floors below, one of the gargoyles was missing. Probably Crosbie was the only person who noticed it.

Once inside, surly as ever, he would grunt to Mackenzie, go into his office, and bang the door. Thank God, that was it over for another week; and in two days' time, it would be Mackenzie's turn. He would have the place to himself. It was as if the Memorial belonged to him, and him alone.

He always went on a tour of inspection after his day off. The museum room was unlit, and he pressed the switch, peering round suspiciously. Everything all right, so far.

Outside, on the first landing, he looked down experimentally. In some ways, this seemed the worst balcony of all. One climbed quickly, fresh on the first shallow flight, and the height came as a shock, people staring up, foreshortened, and the flowerbeds like scraps stuck on to green paper. Higher up, it wasn't so bad. The horizon beckoned over roofs and towers to the sea, and the eye was level, or higher than, the frieze of spires which graced the tilted streets. What lay below was irrelevant, masked by the diminishing pinnacles which, from this height, seemed to angle out and expose the core of the Memorial, the centre stalk, at the tip of which Crosbie stood like a captain on the bridge of his ship.

Like a good captain, he knew every inch of his command. With a batter of wings, a pigeon flapped past him, and this reminded him of the nests below. Cautiously, he leaned over.

Tucked away behind a whirl of stone, the nest lay bare and empty, a bit of broken shell sticking to one corner, and a few smoky feathers fluttering at the bottom. Furious, rushing down the stairs with practised speed, he confronted Mackenzie in his cubby-hole.

'Have you been at thae pigeons?'

'Been at them? What do you mean, *at* them?'

'Interfering wi' them. One of the nest's been herried.'

'Well, I never touched it. Heavens, I could never reach it! Have some sense, Mr Crosbie!'

'Oh, I've sense enough! I know you've never liked them! But just you wait. I'll watch you! You let me see you interfering wi' thae birds, and you'll hear about it. Now, I'm warnin' you!'

'Ach!' Mackenzie gave a quick, half-humorous wave of his hand, and dismissed the whole subject. The old man was getting more crabbit every day. Better to take no heed, and just let him rave.

Muttering, Crosbie went into the museum room. After a night in the motel, the Memorial was like home to him, but he did not relish a day of patrolling the winding stairs and balconies. It was tiring work keeping the people moving, harrying them up, and then coaxing them down. They all wanted to cluster at the top and pick out landmarks, and this caused jams on the stairs.

Today, the public were more annoying than usual. One woman, in the dark bit where there was hardly room to squeeze past, suddenly announced that she had claustrophobia, and began to scream, so that her husband had to help her down, hysterical and protesting, upsetting all the other people who also felt that the stairs were too dark and too narrow, but who were bravely trying to hide their fear. He caught a youth chalking a small arrow and the word UP at one of the concealed entrances, and gave him a lecture about defacing public property. 'Well, it's true, innit?' argued the youth. 'People get lost. You should have signs up,' and he tossed the chalk over the side. That was a particularly dangerous thing to do. In cases like this, the drill was to order the offender down; but how, thought Crosbie, do you get a person off the Memorial in a crush like this? The public seemed to be siding with the wrongdoer. Mackenzie would have handled it better, no doubt; but when Mackenzie was on duty up here, he, Crosbie, would be bent double, pushing tickets through a small window . . .

You couldn't win.

And then he saw the child, leaning recklessly over the balustrade.

She was a thin child, in a long, rather old-fashioned pink frock, with her hair strained back in a sort of Alice in Wonderland style. At that moment, nobody was with her. As he looked, he saw that she was trying to get a leg over the balustrade. He noticed all this in the few petrified seconds before he sprinted silently towards her, hands out, and then – there was nobody there. Half afraid – surely she couldn't have toppled, in the instant of his eyes shutting in terror? – he forced himself to look over, but he could see nothing, no body lying, all blood and broken joints, no crowds hiding their eyes from horror. All he saw was a pigeon on a pinnacle, with empty space behind it; and all at once he felt a white weakness sweep over him, a sudden realization of the height, and the danger of his own position. He felt himself fall, slow, slow, the breathless dunt as he struck projecting stone, the long, drift down, the streaked galleries flashing past as if he were rushing down in a lift, floor after floor, and yet taking a long, long time . . . Sick, he

recovered himself, pushed himself away from the balustrade, and tottered to meet the batch who were coming up.

'Which of youse has got a wee girl with you? A wee girl
in a pink frock?'

Nobody seemed to have an answer.

'Well, watch her,' he grumbled. 'Do you want to get me
into trouble? Weans is not allowed up unaccompanied.'

Two days later he saw her again – but at night.

He often prowled about at night, taking a last look over
the city before he settled to his somewhat uncomfortable
rest. On a clear night, lights traced the blackness like lurex
thread, lights twinkling for miles and miles, right over to the
sea where, even there, an odd flash lit the water. He liked
the scene, but it humbled him. The lights meant nothing to
him. He was lonely, apart from them, shut up in a tower
because there was nowhere for him to go. Even the pigeons
were asleep.

And then the child came up to him, not near, but near
enough to be seen in the reflected shine of the city lights.

'Hello,' she said.

Crosbie glowered at her, mindful first of all of the rule
book.

'What are you doing here? The Memorial closes at six
o'clock.'

'I live here,' she said.

'No, you don't. Nobody lives here.' He almost said,
'except me', but he stopped himself in time.

'I've lived here for years. Longer than you.'

So she knew, then? Warily, in case he gave himself away,
he decided not to press the point.

'Come on, now. You'll need to get down. I'll let you out.'

'I don't want out. I can't *get* out. I'm going to stay here
for ever and ever.'

'Oh no, you're not. You're going down that stair—'

'You can't make me.' She moved to the balustrade, and,
hastily, he changed his tone.

'Come on down to the museum room. It's nice there. I'll put on the electric fire, and we'll have a cup of tea.'

For a minute, she considered, and then she was past him, teasingly, spiralling down in the dark, sure-footed, and into the room before him. He looked at her, droll, old-fashioned, and hesitated with the kettle in his hand.

'Will your mother not be looking for you?'

The face clouded. 'No.' She sounded more childish now, less sure of herself. 'She's – I don't know where she is. She's dead.'

Something about the way she said it, the way she phrased it, sounded strange. Once more he hesitated, puzzled.

'Well, who looks after you, then?'

'Nobody.' A little inconsequential shrug. 'I'm on my own here. Ever since I got killed.'

'*Killed?*'

'I fell over, into the gardens. Years ago. Long before you were here.'

'Any more of that daft talk and out you go. You shouldn't be here in the first place.'

'But it's true! See yon broken gargoyle? That was me. I struck it coming down.'

'Away and don't be daft. You—'

'But I did! Long ago. They never mended it. The edge isn't so sharp now. If you weren't such a stupid old man you'd have seen me before this.'

'You mean you're a . . . ?'

'Aye, I'm a ghost. You cannie catch me, for a wee bawbee . . . !'

And he couldn't. It was not that she was intangible, only that she seemed always to elude him. Slowly, he came to terms with the facts; one, that the Memorial was haunted, and two, that Mackenzie must never know.

It was the beginning of a new life for him. Lonely, inarticulate and homeless, he found himself looking forward to seeing the child, lying awake, waiting for her to come, exasperated when she kept him waiting.

Jean, she was called. Just Jean. That was all he could find out. She was a sorry, neglected little creature, only half-clad, her dress not nearly warm enough for the nippy autumn days, and he worried about her, sharp and wan with the cold. She was vulnerable, too. A word could send her lips quivering, and more than once he had reduced her to tears.

She was such a little brat! Her fingers were into everything, she poked and fiddled and answered back when he checked her. Many a time he felt that she would be the better of a good smacked bottom – she had fallen to her death, he discovered, by sheer showing off and disobedience – but how can you smack a ghost? She gloried in it, tantalizing him, at the same time as she seemed to yearn, sometimes, wistfully, for a little petting, a little human contact.

'What was it like,' he asked her once, 'when you ... ?'

She seemed to concentrate. 'All dark and fast, and bright lights ... and ... I knew it was past, and couldn't happen again, ever ...'

He had a feeling she was sorry it had happened.

She grudged him his days off. For some reason or other, she refused to show herself to Mackenzie. 'Don't go,' she said. 'If you liked me, you'd stay.' He felt that it would be a relief to get away from her clinging demands, but all through his long days of freedom he found himself thinking of her, trying to placate her. Sheepishly, he went into stores and bought clothes for her, clothes that he selected himself from the counters, judging her size, and guessing what she should wear. He brought them back in his suitcase, white cotton pants, coloured bobby-sox, warm slippers with bunny faces on them, and he laid them out, hoping she might take them, and put them on ...

But she didn't, or couldn't, he never knew which. Nor did she taste the lollipops or sherbert dabs he bought to tempt her. She wasn't like a real child at all, except in her almost malicious teasing. 'You cannie catch me, for a wee bawbee ...' She eluded him, shrill and swift and tempting.

And then, one day, Mackenzie found the clothes lying in the office.

Crosbie was growing careless – or was it Jean who had left the door open? He didn't know. Mackenzie's excuse was that he wanted more tickets. He came in and saw the child's knickers, the bunny slippers, and a pile of coloured comics and cheap necklaces. So *that* was how the dirty old devil spent his time . . . ?

'. . . for a niece of mine,' mumbled Crosbie, but he knew Mackenzie didn't believe him. And what else could he say? 'Knock next time you come in!' he shouted. 'You've no bloody business in here!'

Things were going to pieces. There was less trust than ever between him and Mackenzie, and Jean was beginning to tire him out. He couldn't stand the long, exhausting days and the nights when she kept him from sleeping. Desperate, he was driven to make one more attempt to find lodgings, somewhere he could have a little peace; anywhere, no matter how expensive, so long as he could make ends meet at the end of the week, and call the place his own.

So here he was, wandering along again at the pace of the crowd, staring at the shop windows all decked for the tourist. Bright maps concertinaed together to direct him, picture postcards revolved on stands, floral dotted parks, pillared ruins under a blue sky. The Memorial was a great favourite, its lacy spires snapped in sunshine, always in sunshine, its vital statistics in a wedge of print at the back. George Crosbie knew these statistics off by heart.

Forced to the inside of the pavement, he could not take his eyes from the shops. Idly, he read down the list of tartans, picturing himself, ludicrously, in a kilt. He stared at honey jars and boxes of rock, antique chairs and clerical gowns. No, it wouldn't do. He cut across the park, on the side farthest from the Memorial, and climbed the steep streets to the old town. Things would be cheaper here. Maybe there would be lodgings to spare.

But the old town, historical, picturesque, had also been tarted up and made trendy for tourism. The shops were cluttered with skean-dubhs and cameos, cairngorms and old

Masonic medals, and they served exotic meals in expensively converted tenements. Down a close he saw the Memorial, its topmost balcony crawling with people. It was as if he was tied to it, circling as a dog circles a tree on the end of his chain. His loose lip drooping, he turned away and watched a one-man band clash and gyrate along the gutter, a man making himself ridiculous for the sake of a few coppers. 'I could be worse,' he thought. 'I could be like that.'

He turned away, walking further and further, till the sun went in, and it grew grey towards teatime. Here, the streets were shabby, the shops small and cluttered, bargains painted on the windows with white paint. He began to knock on doors. Landings smelled of bacon and kippers and sliced sausage, and, greasy lips, still chewing, said *no*. It was a bad time to ask. He tramped up and down so many stairs, saw grey yards from dusty landing windows, and stroked thin cats ingratiatingly. No one would take him in.

When at last he found someone who had a room, and was willing to let it, he was too tired to be particular about the price. He paid a week in advance, and sat stiffly on the bed, taking his boots off. It was what he called a posh bed, with a gold-quilted cover with a nylon frill, and the landlady told him he was expected to take it off. He agreed, agreed to everything. There was a bedside lamp, a cheap chest of drawers, and a cupboard for his clothes. Somewhere to come home to at night . . . his landlady had hinted, too, that for a small extra charge she might see to his washing.

Lying on two pillows, with the blankets tucked in, he couldn't sleep for sheer comfort. He lay awake, too, worrying about Jean. Maybe she would cry tonight, left on her own. It was a lonely life for her. She was just a bairn, after all, and surely a bairn shouldn't have to suffer so long . . . ? Maybe, at Sunday School, they had told her that she would go to Hell if she didn't behave, and she hadn't believed it.

Hell was leaving a child alone in the Memorial, year after weary year. Mercy tempered it a little by the companionship of an old grouch like Crosbie . . .

'I'll see her in the morning,' he consoled himself, as he fell asleep with the clock ticking on for three.

She was angry at being left; tearful at first, huddled away in misery, and then spiteful, like the little brat that she was. In the half-hour before the Memorial opened to the public, she riled him till his hand itched to slap her, but something, pity, or guilt, he didn't know what, made him try to conciliate her. She wasn't used to his mildness, and it maddened her more. Desperately, she drew on powers that frightened even herself. Watching him wickedly, with her red tongue going lick, lick round her mouth, she let herself over the balustrade, and . . . walked, floated, she couldn't quite explain it, down to where the pigeons snuggled in a cave of sooty stone. Crosbie, his mouth loose with shock, saw her lift the birds from their nest, and slowly, one by one, thraw their necks, rummle the nest to rubbish, and chuck the lot down to the grass beneath.

He went for her then, straight down to where she stood on nothing, laughing at him, straight down as he had seen it happen before, the streaked galleries flashing past, gargoyle and turret and pinnacle, the sooty carvings and the weathered stone, down and down . . .

'I'll be like her,' he thought. 'For ever and ever—' and then, in a rueful flash, 'and I've paid my room, a week in advance . . .'

He didn't die. They kept him in the Infirmary, and did all they could for him, and then they sent him out, legless, on a little wooden platform on wheels. He became quite adept at propelling it along among the tourists, and the tourists found him almost an attraction. 'Ah well,' they sighed, comfortably, dropping the odd coin into his hat, and thinking of their own niggling afflictions, 'you always see somebody worse off than yourself!'

Crosbie lives now in the Working Men's Hotel; permanently. It is cheap and handy, and there are people there who

are willing to carry him up the stairs and give him hints on
how to capitalize on his disabilities. This is where he learned
to carry with him a small melodeon. He doesn't play, but
from time to time he moves it open and shut, tunelessly.
It's better than begging. It looks as if he's making an effort,
and the tourists like that; and it makes up for the surliness
of his attitude. If he were less surly, more of an extrovert,
he could make a good thing out of publicizing the fact that
he got his injuries falling off the top of the Memorial; but
probably they wouldn't believe him.

He has a lot to put up with. Frustration is the worst of his
troubles. Once the one-man band went by, banging and
blasting away splendidly, knees going, elbows going, drums
and cymbals and mouth organ all in a crashing medley of
noise. Crosbie envied him. You have to be fit to be a one-
man band.

Then there are the pigeons. They waddle past him, fat
lilac birds, on their way to where another man feeds them,
and makes a grand display of it. Children feed them too,
buying packets of stuff from a vendor in the gardens. None
of them are *his* pigeons; none of them care. His own birds
stick to the Memorial, and never come near him.

Perhaps worst of all is the torment of watching the
Memorial. With a genius for self-punishment, he has
stationed himself where he can see all that goes on. All day
the visitors inch and crawl along the balconies; all day
Mackenzie jollies them along; but at night (and he sits at his
pitch long after the Memorial has emptied) he sees the child
flitting about, the pink frock pitifully worn, the long hair
floating. Sometimes she cries for him, sobbing for him to
come back, promising to be a good girl if he'll only come
up and speak to her. At other times, he will hear her teasing
him, taunting him, with an artless invitation to play.

> 'You cannie catch me
> For a wee bawbee . . .'

THE CURSE OF MATHAIR NAN UISGEACHAN

My childhood was scattered and quite lonely. When asked, 'Where are you from?', I answered, 'Scotland', without much conviction. I enjoyed the nomadic independence of an emotional refugee. I was lucky.

My grandparents owned large estates in the Highlands. Fertile valley pastures were farmed or let to tenants and the rest divided into crofts, deer forests and moorland. At a tender age I was initiated to the rites of aristocratic modes and manners, what I should and should not do, who I should and should not speak to, what I must and must not wear, why it was forbidden to play with the gardener's son in the nursery but tolerated in the servants' hall. Once old enough to express my feelings I made my parents understand that I did not relish such restrictive practices. Memories of the castle marred the pleasure of Highland holidays, rooms cold and dusky even in the middle of the day, no central heating, a private electricity supply working off the burn and dungeons cold as caves oozing snail wine over pitted flags.

One of my aunts was drowned on the morning of her tenth birthday and both my uncles were killed in the war, a tragedy that deeply affected my grandparents. My mother admitted that other families suffered as much without resorting to extremes of morbid self-accusation.

'Perhaps the contrast was too great,' she said. 'As children we were especially happy.'

There were five, all of whom excelled at one thing or another. London society of the '30s was dominated by their charm and beauty, and throughout those doomed and brilliant summers the castle was filled with friends from the south. There was shooting, fishing, stalking, sailing on the sea loch, endless games and parties.

I remember the shadows of trees lengthening across the leafy lawn in autumn and thinking that the castle itself would be swallowed in darkness so that the inner dark would meet the outer dark and together create a blackness unknown even in the vaults of Egypt. It was then that I became frightened and stayed close to the fire.

My grandfather died while I was still at Oxford. He was seventy-two. My cousin, Hugh, son of the eldest uncle, inherited. He was six years older than me and worked for a merchant bank in Toronto. He came home immediately, bringing his Canadian wife, Anne. My grandmother left and went to live in Aberdeenshire with my aunt Magda.

I heard snatches of gossip here and there. Anne's renovation of the castle, Hugh's plans for the estate, rumours of an interest in deer farming, something not attempted outside Scandinavia, causing disquiet amongst the local gentry who expected invitations to stalk during the season. Obviously Hugh was having none of that. It sounded encouraging.

Hugh had been brought up by his mother in Hampshire and had spent even less time in Scotland than I. An extraordinary likeness to his father upset my grandmother so much that instead of seeing him she wrote copious letters explaining everything that was going on so that he would know, if nothing else, the names of the estate workers and what jobs they did. Hugh told me later that he filed these letters without opening them so that when my grandfather died he brought them out and laid them across the floor of his flat in Toronto and opened every third one.

'I spent six and a half hours on that bloody floor,' he said. 'By the end I could tell you the name of the stonemason's son-in-law and why the joiner's wife couldn't have children. I knew who was a good worker, who was a bad worker, who poached salmon, who snared pheasants, what was planted in the garden, when and by whom, the condition of the cook's varicose veins before and after her operation. Of course, when I arrived and met them they were very impressed.'

I contacted Hugh a week before leaving Oxford and asked whether I could stay for a summer at the shepherd's bothy on the loch. He thought it an excellent idea and said that I could stay for as long as I liked. He seemed genuinely pleased to hear from me.

Spring comes late in the Highlands and when it does it is less dramatic than the sensual bursting of wet buds in rural England. Winter hangs deep in the hills long into April and May and there are moments when you imagine the dead land will remain forever still. But when the green shoots push up through the white stalks and wild flowers pierce damp hussocks beside the river and along the shores of the loch it is more wondrous in its miracle because the need for reassurance is essential to combat the harsh realities. Beyond the castle towards the western regions the land is barren and bleak, fearful with a grandeur that defies beauty. The lost trees of the old forest lie white and rotting against the brown grass. Eagles and hoodies, deer and foxes live there; no people. Once this glen, and others like it, were filled with thriving communities. Now the heartland is a forgotten wilderness. Even in the eyes of crofters who reside at the outer reaches of the loch you can sense a wound going back so far, an agony of the soul unchecked by whisky, state charity or tourism. The dark lines of this nation's dead scar the earth, if not in fact, certainly in spirit. Even Hugh, the new laird and chief of the clan, knew that what existed once, a tribal system based on communal enterprise and sharing, owing all and yet owning all, had passed away. He was a rich man, a farmer. He played the role, wore the kilt.

'It is expected of me,' he said.

I laughed, remembering my early lessons in the nature of duty.

Anne and Hugh had taken care over the work they had done at the castle. I felt the emphasis had changed. Anne, being Canadian, was free from the strictures of the English upper class. She was energetic and conscientious, eager to learn and understand. They had plans, not only for deer farming which had begun already on a limited scale, but for the renovation of derelict cottages and the building of chalets as holiday homes, the opening of a shop in the village to encourage weavers and potters and craftsmen of all sorts, and the possible construction of a deep freeze unit and smoking house so that salmon could be dressed and frozen direct from the river.

I settled into the bothy. Although an outsider I was surprised by the reception I received from so many of the estate workers who remembered my visits as a child. To them I was a member of the old family, more so than Hugh who appeared too modern with his ambitious ideas and foreign wife. I tried to reassure them by expressing my enthusiasm. They smiled, nodded, but remained suspicious. The situation was intriguing. I waited and watched. Spring faded into summer and the hot blue days when the wind fluttered in the trees and deer wandered to the river in the early evening filled with a timeless sense of life's slow evolution, trout jumping in the loch, martins diving and soaring about the eaves, bats jagged against the moon, the zing of insects, chirp of small birds in the reeds, midges rising out of the marshes like clouds of dusty pollen.

The bothy was four miles from the castle, up the track that followed the loch half its length along the northern shore. No shepherd had lived there since the war although the building remained strong with thick stone walls and a slate roof already green with moss. I had a Rayburn stove in which I burnt sticks and coal, and a room beyond with a bed and a chest of drawers and a cupboard. From my door I could see where the loch turned west in the shape of an L and the mountain cut sheer into the water. At that point, below the cliff, was the Mathair Nan Uisgeachan whirlpool, an extraordinary natural fault, capable of dragging down swimming stags. At the cliff face was a cavern leading to a narrow underwater channel and when the wind blew from the south-west the spin of the pool was wider than the length of a tall pine tree. Anne tried to persuade Hugh to let frogmen go down to discover the distance of the channel and where it emerged. Hugh would placate her with vague promises but I knew nothing would come of it.

My life adapted to the quiet run of the days. I dug a small

vegetable garden at the front of the bothy and wired the sheep pen for chickens. I bought a secondhand chainsaw and an old van and spent the bright still afternoons when fishing was impossible cutting wood for the stove. Twice a week I dined at the castle and occasionally Anne and Hugh would picnic at the loch and we'd take the boat out. I did not question the relevance of my existence or allow myself to brood on the future. I was twenty-two, had spent the last fifteen years at schools and university. I knew I wanted to write and as the weeks passed became more and more convinced of what this should be. I kept a diary of thoughts and ideas that occurred to me during the day and soon a pattern emerged, two themes simultaneously recurring. The first was my impression of the land itself, the emptiness of the wilderness area. The second concerned the family, my mother's childhood filled with joy and promise, followed so fast by a desperate sadness. Somewhere these two themes connected.

Hugh spent his time in the estate office with Roger Cornish, my grandfather's factor. The difficulty of creating change in a system that had worked for years on the basis that every conversation must be prefaced with lengthy inquiries about the health of each member of a man's family was hard enough, especially for Hugh who understood the rudiments of North American efficiency. There was no sense of urgency, no desire for innovation. The soft underbelly of feudalism, combined with a romantic notion of clannish brotherhood, enhanced the status quo and made progress erratic. Roger had given up the struggle and was content to let things follow their own course. He was an Englishman whose ambitions did not extend far beyond his salmon rod, his twelve-bore and a full case of rare malt whisky. Locally he was well liked. He turned a blind eye to the evasions that were perpetrated in the name of the estate. 'A little honest poaching never ruined a river,' he would say. 'And if the stalkers are selling the odd beast during hind season, God knows they aren't paid much!' As long as discretion was maintained and a certain restraint exercised, why make a fuss? It was only when outsiders intervened, poachers from the south with tins of Cimag and high velocity rifles, that Roger, the police and the stalkers acted together.

'That's as it should be,' he told me. 'We don't want the Mafia here.'

'This *is* the Mafia,' I said.

He poured another of his mature Highland malts and passed me the glass.

'You're in a unique position to observe the discrepancies of an archaic system,' he said. 'But don't get it into your head that change is always for the best. I know the problems of these people. They come and tell me. I know who is operating an illegal still, who is taking dole money and working jobs on the side. That's not important compared with retaining an understanding so that life can operate to the best advantage of all concerned. The Highlander is a proud and independent chap, cunning as a fox, I'll grant you, but he has to be, he knows that, and he takes care whom he trusts, if he trusts anyone. He trusts us, or rather uses us, but that's all right because I recognize his loyalty remains first towards himself and secondly towards the continuation of his way of life. You can't tell a Highlander what he *should* be doing, how much money he *should* be making. He won't listen. Why should he? Now Hugh is talking of putting up the crofters' rents. It's madness. I don't care how absurd it may seem to someone fresh out of Harvard, or wherever it was, but for the people themselves it's an insult because they feel that land belongs to them, which it did in the old days. And look at the politics. Where else do you find Liberals winning seats? Lloyd George is dead and gone. You wouldn't know it. The younger generation think they're *anti*-Establishment, *against* authority. The Highlander *invented* the word! You must accept that from the start or you'll find they're agin you.'

Hugh was easing Roger out by taking more and more responsibility himself. He imported an accountant from Edinburgh to go through the books and advise on methods of improving office efficiency. Obviously money was being borrowed and not repaid, rents lapsed unaccountably, bad debts carried over for years without complaint, files disintegrated into a series of scrawled cross-references and notes from Roger written in an indecipherable hand on the sleeves of envelopes. Hugh called it 'a miser's den of hoarded waste'. The accountant stayed six weeks before departing in a state of nervous exhaustion. From this came the third theme of my prospective novel, also connected to the others by a thread of circumstantial invention, the Highlander's jealous hold on the property of his father, a communal distrust of visitors, disguised by guileful charm, passions lying at the heart of pride, already damaged by history and now directed towards the breakdown of progressive change.

Anne was forever arranging bazaars and charity evenings, organizing the tourist shop, supervising the renovation of the cottages and planning sites for the chalets. Everything was contained in that bright smile, the *immediacy* of response, so that enthusiasms appeared less sincere than actual, encouraging noises to satisfy the curiosity of the natives. In June she caught a virulent flu bug and went to bed. Hugh asked me to drop by if I had the time and cheer her up. I did so. She talked of a belief in positive thinking, the act of creating atmosphere for constructive relationships, and confided that there were days when she came home and wept with frustration. I found her awkward, strangely uncertain.

'I guess I'm naive,' she said. 'But sometimes I want to stand on a table at one of those damned meetings and pull off my clothes just to *force* some kind of response.'

She laughed.

'You must think I'm crazy,' she said.

She was embarrassed.

'It sounds very sane to me,' I said.

'Hugh would be devastated,' she said.

I told her about my novel and the problems of the conflicting themes.

'You're *right*,' she said. 'I used to spend hours *marvelling* at that beautiful thing, you know? The mountains and the

water and the sky. The peace of it. The real open *space*.
It intoxicated me.' She laughed again. 'But when I walk
alone with the dogs, which I do whenever I can, I recognize
what you're saying. It's like I'm a stranger in a foreign land.'

'You are,' I said. 'So am I.'

'Sure, but then you feel this oppression.'

'Yes.'

'I feel it too, but differently. I feel *surrounded*. Like I'm
not alone.'

The good weather broke and the rain returned, dark grey
days when clouds hung low over the hills, creeping into the
glen like pillows of damp hay. Anne waited for me. It was
always the same. I arrived for lunch and we spent the afternoons together, sitting in front of the fire in the drawing-
room, talking or playing backgammon. She said that she
had been sick more than once and often woke dizzy with
nausea. Hugh was worried. Three weeks after the illness
she seemed depressed and listless.

'I can't interest her in anything,' he said.

One day as I was leaving, the clouds lifted and sun
glistened on the marsh reeds beside the road. Anne squeezed
my arm.

'Let's go out,' she said. 'It's beautiful.'

We took the dogs and walked along the edge of the loch,
across the burn, over to the far side of the river. Water ran
down the hill, through peat hags, under tussocks, breaking
into pools. The sudden heat hatched a plague of midges that
clung to our faces and hands. We began to climb.

'We mustn't go too far,' I said. 'You're tired.'

She looked at me, the sun full on her cheeks. I was aware
how pretty she was.

'You've changed,' I said.

'People don't change,' she said. 'They adapt.'

'What do you mean?'

'I adapt to you.'

'That can't be good.'

'It's good for me.'

The silence embraced us, filling the air with feelings

neither dared to express. I turned and looked back at the castle. She stood close to me now. Her arm touched the rib of my sweater.

'This is mad,' I said.

'I know it's mad,' she said.

I began to walk down the hill. She followed, her small delicate body moving easily over the sodden earth. We came to an open space of clear short grass on a mound beside the river. She stopped.

'I want to show you something,' she said.

She called the dogs. They came bounding out of the peat hags, stopping at the edge of the grass.

'Come on!' she cried.

They circled us, whining, almost on their bellies.

'How did you know?' I asked.

'It's happened before,' she said.

Across the river were the marshy flats leading to the road, and beyond the road, the castle, square and dark against the black trees. Suddenly I felt cold.

Hugh's car appeared round the curve at the edge of the wood. We crossed the river at the shallow ford and waded through the reeds. Midges whined in our ears again. We stood on the gravel path and waited, the dogs panting from their run, tongues dripping. I looked over the river at the grassy knoll.

'What do you think it is?' Anne said.

'I don't know,' I said.

'I want to see you,' she said.

'You *are* seeing me,' I said.

'I want to see you tomorrow.'

'Why?'

'Will you come?'

'I don't know. I don't know if I can.'

'Please.'

We heard Hugh shouting. The dogs scrambled through the rhododendrons, squealing for him. Anne and I walked up the drive. Hugh greeted us.

'How are you?' he called.

She smiled.

'It's time I stopped being an invalid,' she said.

When I arrived the next day as arranged Anne acted as if nothing had happened. I felt confused and hurt. She bustled through lunch, impatient and nervous, busy with details and new plans. I made an excuse and returned to the bothy. I considered packing my suitcase, then and there, but something stopped me, the foolishness of it, the exaggeration on my part of an incident that existed only in my own mind. Escape would defeat its own purpose. Also, I had the notes of my novel. I would devote the remainder of the summer to that.

Two weeks later Hugh told me that Anne was pregnant.

'It'll make all the difference,' he said.

'To what?' I asked.

Already my appreciation of Hugh was waning. He seemed more arrogant than enlightened, more narrow-minded than liberal. His views on what was good for the crofters and the estate did not coincide with local opinion, in fact constantly aggravated it. He wondered why jobs weren't completed on schedule, why everyone had to be told things three times, why the village policeman failed to catch poachers. I could have told him but he wouldn't have listened, and even if he had, wouldn't have believed me.

I walked alone in the hills, spent days fishing on the loch. The interference of mortality was an anachronism. The land was all land, the rocks all rocks. Man's insistence on making his presence felt, showing proof of his existence, was futile against the weight of this wilderness. My sadness, even anger, that communities once prospered in these glens altered as I began to realize that perhaps they did not prosper. Even the ruins of simple steadings were lost. Nothing remained. The silence was not a death in life as I had supposed but a life in death where every living creature was at war.

I worked on the book. It was slow. I felt restless. Why did the mountains oppress me? Why did I nurture five chickens in a wired sheep pen as if their survival was a personal victory?

Anne worried about my isolation.

'What is it?' she asked.

'I don't know,' I said.

She was happy. These were the best days. She would create a sanctuary of love for her baby so that the world outside could be enjoyed with wonder and joy. Again I was struck by the sentimentality of the image.

'I was coming across the hill yesterday, on the other side of the river, and I saw you,' I said.

'Yes,' she said.

'Who was with you?'

'The dogs.'

'There was a girl.'

'He's a boy.' She smiled at me. 'Gypsies are camping at the old sawmill.'

'You like that, don't you?'

'Why?'

'When I first came here I thought you were typical North American—'

'Hey!'

'After adopting stray children you'll be talking to fish.'

'I don't talk any more. I *catch* them. Let's go sometime.'

'All right.'

'When?'

'Next week.'

There was no gypsy camp at the sawmill. I went there and checked and so was surprised to see the child again on the loch shore with Anne when I arrived for the fishing expedition. He was playing in the water beside the boat. He had curly black hair hanging down his shoulders and wore an embroidered white shirt, tied at the waist. He had no shoes. He was very young. Hearing my step on the shingles he darted off into the reeds.

'Hello,' Anne said.

'What's wrong with him?'

'He's shy of men. We both are.'

'I hadn't noticed.'

She kissed me on the cheek.

'Are you a safe sailor?' she asked.

'That depends.'

'On what?'

'Your behaviour.'

She climbed into the boat, taking the rods. I pushed off and jumped in, started the outboard. We sat together as I held the rudder bar, passing Mathair Nan Uisgeachan on the far side and going on towards the west, reaching a bay where a burn dashed down the rocks in a silver waterfall. I cut the engine. We drifted close. I flicked my line free and began to cast. The air was warm. A breeze rippled the surface. There was no sun. We fished twenty yards from the shore, letting the boat glide slowly down with the oars hanging, casting easily with the wind. We caught three trout, all over a pound. The sun came out. The clouds scattered. We landed in a narrow inlet where trees bent at strange angles off the high banks. I opened the picnic basket and we lay in the sun, eating chicken and smoked salmon sandwiches and drinking beer out of bottles. Anne took off her windcheater and sweater. She was not fat yet, still small and slight, dressed in jeans and tee-shirt and shiny red PVC boots. Her blonde hair was cut short, skin freckled and brown from the last spell of fine weather. We talked. She told me what she had missed in her life here, how it frightened her at first and made her borrow habits from her mother, a very organized and dominating woman. She laughed about it now.

'People do that,' I said.

'You don't,' she said.

'I've nothing to lose,' I said.

'You aren't aware of it,' she said, 'but you help me. You have a definite viewpoint which is good. You say, "I don't *care* what they think". Hugh is determined to do what he feels is right and I believe my role is to support and encourage him. But I'm losing out, right down the line, becoming this other person, the one you call "typical North American" like "typical French fries".'

'I didn't mean—'

'Sure, you didn't, but you're right, that's what I am, an unpaid worker in the PR department, no time to sit and discover what it's all about.'

'What is it all about?'

'The baby . . . a whole lot of stuff . . . the future . . .'

'And you feel happy?'

'Don't you?'

I shrugged.

'I don't think about it,' I said.

'Maybe you should.'

I touched her hand. She didn't move.

'Tell me about the book,' she said. I was kneeling, looking down at her. 'I want to know much more about that.'

I kissed her.

'What do you want to know?' I asked.

'Everything,' she said. 'It's not enough, just a little.'

I kissed her ear, her neck.

'Shall I begin at the beginning?' I asked.

She sat up, brushed a hand through her hair.

'The beer's gone to my head,' she said.

'It's gone to mine too.'

'We're on a fishing trip, remember?'

'We've fished. We've done that part.'

'What's the next part?'

'Lying in the grass.'

'We've done that too.'

She turned.

'Let's collect the things together,' she said.

'It's too hot,' I said.

We walked along the side of the hill in the sun. She picked flowers.

A week later I went to stay with Aunt Magda in Aberdeen-shire. It was my grandmother's eightieth birthday and my mother had written from Turkey asking whether I would mind going as neither she nor my father could return for it.

My grandmother was eager to hear all the news. I told
her of Hugh's plans and pretended everything was working
well. I said that I was living at the bothy which seemed
extraordinary to her and that I was writing a novel which
seemed even more extraordinary.

'It's a comedy of manners,' I said, 'set in an imaginary
Highland glen, concerning a group of crippled children in a
big house who become involved with ghosts and goblins
and real policemen in search of an escaped convict who is
pretending to be the spirit of a long dead ancestor.'

'Sounds like a winner,' my uncle said.

On my last evening, when we were alone, Aunt Magda
referred to the novel again and said, 'I'm surprised you
aren't tackling something more serious.'

'It is serious,' I said.

'Goblins?' she said.

'I had to say *something*,' I said.

'What's it really about?' she asked.

I explained the conflicting themes, how their connection
affected the way things happened. My own experience at the
castle was a good example. When I stayed there as a child I
had hated it although wasn't aware until later what it had
been like for her and my mother, what fun they had had. All
I knew was the feeling of my grandparents' disapproval and
resentment which contributed to an atmosphere of perman-
ent gloom, not resentment against me but against life itself,
the cruelties of fate and inexplicable tragedy of the world.

Aunt Magda listened politely. She thought my analysis
naive although didn't say so directly. They had lived in the
nursery as much as I, the only difference being there were
more of them. She did not believe that her mother and father
had been hardened by their children's deaths. They were
hard from the start.

'You've destroyed my thesis,' I said.

'Of course I haven't,' she said. 'You're writing *fiction*.'

It was then that I asked about Fiona, the sister who
drowned.

'Do you ever question your mother?' she asked.

'Sometimes,' I said.

'What does she tell you?'

'She changes the subject.'

'Perhaps she wants to protect you.'

'She said Fiona was rather sad.'

'She had lovely hair, I remember. She was very imaginative and scatter-brained. But I suspect that was less true of her character than a way of avoiding our parents' displeasure. Being the eldest she was made responsible and in order to avoid those constrictions acted incompetent and vague. She was far from incompetent, in fact. She only pretended to be. When my mother wanted her to do a chore or take a message and she was nowhere to be found we said, "She's playing with Lochlan.' My mother thought Lochlan was one of the village children and, of course, that upset her. We weren't supposed to play with the village children or even speak to them. But Fiona insisted that Lochlan lived with us. He was there in the castle. We said, "Why doesn't he play with us?", and she said, "He doesn't like playing with lots of people. He only likes playing with me." We knew he was one of her imaginary friends and didn't think about it but my mother insisted on meeting him. Fiona said he wouldn't come, he was frightened. In the end my mother gave up and we left it at that. One day I met Lochlan. I was tremendously surprised. I had been in the kitchen garden picking strawberries for lunch. Your mother was there too but she was faster than me and had gone on ahead. I wandered back through the rhododendron wood when suddenly I came across Fiona sitting in a tree. There was someone else with her. It looked like a boy, a young boy. I remember he had white clothes. He seemed to be wearing a dress. He was like a boy pretending to be a girl. He had long hair like a girl. But he had a boy's face and when he saw me he scrambled through the branches and down to the ground and ran off into the bushes. I stood there amazed. I was only six. I didn't know what was happening. Fiona started throwing fir-cones at me. She was furious. I began to cry. Fiona climbed down and took my basket and we walked

home together through the bushes. She made me swear not
to tell Mama, or anyone. She said, "Swear you didn't see
Lochlan." I didn't know he *was* Lochlan. Finding out like
that gave me quite a turn. I swore anyway and then a few
weeks later it was Fiona's birthday. What we did on birth-
days was pile presents on the person's plate so that when they
arrived for breakfast there they all were, a huge mound of
presents, tied with coloured ribbons and string. The presents
were opened in front of everyone. Fiona disliked that because it was too public. She disliked Christmas for the same
reason. Emotions were too precious to be made fun of.'

She put her hands in her lap, rubbed them together
slowly.

'I was sharing a room with Fiona and on that morning,
the morning of her birthday, she woke early and began putting on her clothes. There was a noise, I don't know what
now, she dropped a shoe or something, and I awoke and saw
her half-dressed. I told her she couldn't leave, it was her
birthday and we had presents, *everyone*! She said that was
the reason she was getting up early. She didn't want to
disappoint us. She was going to meet Lochlan. He had a
present for her too and she couldn't disappoint him either.
If I hadn't seen Lochlan I would have known she was telling
lies. But I *had* seen him and I thought, perhaps he *has* got a
present for her. It was awful. I didn't know what to do.
Fiona held my hands and said, "Dear Magda, you must
believe me because it's true." I made her promise to be back
in time. She said she would. I was full of trepidation. I
couldn't *understand* Lochlan. I couldn't *imagine* him quite,
his life, where he came from, why he looked like he did. But
I trusted Fiona. She was so much older, so much on her
own. We waited at the breakfast table, my father and
mother, the servants, Nanny, all the children. I knew she
would have returned if she could. Something must have
stopped her. I couldn't think what. My mother took me outside and tried to force me to say where she had gone, but I
wouldn't. I was sent to my room. I stayed there all morning.
The doors were locked and no one was allowed to come in.

Our Nanny brought me some food at lunch-time. Fiona was still missing. Nanny said, "You don't know where she is, do you?" I said, "No." She said, "Do you think she's run away?" I said, "She wouldn't run away, she promised." Nanny was a very patient and long-suffering woman. She said Fiona was in danger and only I could help. But it was too late. One of the gillies brought her body back. He had found her in the river.'

'Did you discover about Lochlan?' I asked.

'He must have been a tinker's child,' she said. 'There used to be a number of people like that in those days, travelling the roads, selling things. Some were gypsies. Others were tinkers. We liked the tinkers best. They told wonderful stories and weren't frightening like the gypsies. Often when we went into the kitchen to see cook there might be a tinker sitting at the table, having a meal or a cup of tea. They loved children and made a great fuss of us. I remember they smelt of horses. I remember that most of all, their smell. Cook wouldn't have gypsies in because she said they had powers. We wanted to know what these powers were and longed to meet one to find out. But cook was wrong because tinkers were rogues, very charming and sweet, a bit like the Irish, but not very trustworthy.'

Already it was dark. We were sitting in the small drawing-room and neither of us had thought of switching on a light. The fire glowed with the embers of logs lit two hours earlier.

The door opened and my uncle entered.

'What are you two plotting?' he said.

'We had no idea it was so late,' Aunt Magda said.

Next morning I left early and arrived in the village before lunch. Roger was at the office. He said that Hugh wouldn't be coming in today, he was visiting the crofters. I drove up the glen, past the bare foundations of the freezing factory, into the hills. I saw no one. Silence gathered in the blowing grasses although the hum of the motor was a sound enclosed within its vacuum. The castle was empty. I waited. No one came. I drove on to the bothy. Plates in the sink had been washed and stacked on the shelf. My bed was made with new linen, clothes folded in the chest of drawers. The floor was scrubbed and dusted. I changed into old cords and sweater, pulled on my boots and went out to feed the hens. I noticed that the garden had been weeded. I walked down to the loch. The boat was gone. I wandered along the shore on the near side, following the track. The wind was blustery but not cold, the sun flashing between clouds. I walked two miles to where the track climbed into the heather above Mathair Nan Uisgeachan. I rested in a hussock of grass. The loch curved away to the west and I could see almost its whole length. I searched for the boat. It was not there. The waters roared below me. I clambered down and peered over the rock. I saw the boat, spinning in the whirlpool, its oars missing, Anne's red boots and windcheater awash under the seat. I knelt on the cliff top, unable to move, spray spitting, bursting into my face. As I watched the boat sank. It happened very fast. I crawled back into the heather. I was breathing hard. I stood up and walked along the northern shore. The dark hills grew darker. I shouted, my voice dying in the air. I could have walked to the sea, it would have made no difference. A bird cried over the water, a shrill high squeal. The wind dropped. I returned, hurrying along the path. When I reached the bothy, night had fallen. I took the van and drove to the castle. The lights were on, the drawing-room door open. Hugh sat in the chair beside the fire, reading a newspaper. His eyes were stone. I said, Anne's dead. He said, oh yes. He was calm and distant like a man glimpsed through the window of a moving train. We collected brandy from the store cupboard and blankets from the chest on the landing. The moon was full. In the stables was an old boat strapped to the frame of a trailer. We reversed the Land Rover and fixed it to the bar. Oars were standing against the wall. I slipped them in with the rowlocks. Hugh carried the spare outboard across from the garage and I collected a can of petrol. We drove to the loch, unhitched the trailer in the water. Hugh screwed the outboard down and filled it with petrol. I pushed the boat off, using one of the oars as a punt pole. Hugh started the

engine. I sat at the front. Hugh steered. The light was silvery
grey against the black shadows of the shore. We kept close,
moved slowly. I watched the line of rocks and grass, the
contours of peat walls. We stopped to investigate a sub-
merged tree trunk. Hugh shouted, listened, shouted again.
Waves lapped the bottom of the boat. We continued up the
loch. Hugh's face was a skull. Four hinds bounded away
from one of the burns. We stopped again in a bay two miles
beyond the turn. I opened the brandy and we drank. Wind
rippled across the water. It was colder now. We seemed to
wait for hours. Neither of us spoke. Hugh started the engine
and turned into the centre of the loch. The wind was sharper,
waves rolling past. I huddled in my sweater. Hugh steered
towards Mathair Nan Uisgeachan. I expected him to pull
away and take us down the last stretch to where the Land
Rover stood on the beach. But he didn't. He kept going. In
the distance I heard a growling roar. I looked over. We
were close to the rocks. I could see spray bursting up the
wall. Hugh cut the engine and we drifted. I jumped for the
oars, rammed them in, pushed hard, forcing us to stop. I
felt the tug of the whirlpool against the wooden spars. I
pulled with all my strength. We seemed stuck. The boat
began to twist, the shiny rocks loomed above. I fought with
the oars. I couldn't see Hugh. He was behind me. I heard
the engine whine. The boat rocked. We broke free. The
engine stopped again. I turned. Hugh was staring at the pool.
Something was down there, struggling in the water. I saw
tiny white arms. It was the gypsy child. The boat drifted
closer. I screamed. The child spun in the spiral, white shirt
billowing like a flower. Hugh threw off his jacket. I caught
him by the waist. The boat tipped and plunged. Hugh
pushed me back and I fell against the seat. The boat bent
with the spin, water flooding us. I jerked a rowlock from its
pinion. Hugh was about to dive. I hit him on the side of the
head and he dropped. The boat was half-full of water. I
grasped the starting handle and pulled. The engine caught. I
gave it full throttle. The boards shivered. Suction held us.
The engine squealed, roared, and the boat jumped, slewing

wide into broken water beyond the hole. I steered into
shingle at the corner where the burn came in, stopped the
engine and pulled the blades up before striking stones. I
helped Hugh on to the bank. We were soaked to the skin.
He moaned. I held him. He was weaker now, his breath
gasping, lips stretched, eyes bulging like eggs. I pushed him
up the hill. He stumbled. Whisps of cloud shaded the moon.
The air was icy. I touched Hugh's arm. It was stiff as wood.
The child was standing beside the boat. He ran towards us.
Hugh lifted him into his arms. The child clung to his neck. I
could not speak. My mind was frozen. Hugh walked to the
loch. He pushed the boat out. I fell to my knees. The sky
opened. I saw birds flying across the sun. I was in an aeroplane over a desert. The desert was blue like the sea although
it wasn't the sea. There were palm trees and caravans of
camels and sand dunes stretching across the whole length of
the earth. Suddenly the engines spluttered and coughed and
we began to descend. I was alone. There was no one else in
the aeroplane. I walked through to the front to find the
pilot but there was no pilot. I sat at the controls. I pulled the
joystick. The plane steadied and began to glide. Behind me
I heard the sound of sobbing. I looked through the cabin
door. Anne was sitting in one of the seats. I wanted to comfort her and yet couldn't leave the controls. I watched the
sand dunes coming up at me. At last, before the crash came,
I turned to run but tripped and fell through the floor. I was
in a room with white walls. I heard the sobbing quite clearly.
A woman stood at the window. She was small. She seemed
very old. I asked where I was and she said, you mustn't distress yourself. She brought me soup in a bowl. I drank the soup.
Everything became dim. I was in the courtyard of the castle,
ringing the bell of the cook's flat. It was night and the moon
was shining. No one answered. I walked out on to the
road and the child was with me. I said, I didn't forget you.
He smiled, resting against my shoulder. There was blood on
his hands and arms. I said, we'll go to the river and wash it
off. But the old woman stood in my path. I laid the child in
the grass and went with her. She said, you're safe now. I re-

membered the child and said we must find him because he'll awake and feel afraid. The old woman said, we shall talk about that in the morning. The room was full of sun. The old woman stood at the window, looking out. I thought, all this has happened before. I am dreaming. I am no longer alive and my dreams are repeating themselves. I asked whether we had talked about the child and she said, yes, and came and sat on a chair beside my bed. Her voice had a lilting softness and yet her face was scarred with grief. I said, let me touch your hand. She said, no, that you must never do. Then she told me the story. She said, once two brothers lived at the castle. Roderick, the elder, married the daughter of the Lord of the Isles, a beautiful fair girl called Shona. Calum, the younger, was forever racing through the forests, hunting day and night. He was the best horseman, a fearless warrior. Roderick was strong, a leader. He was chief of the clan. In time, a child was born, a son. During the feast of celebration a woman approached Roderick and told him the child was not his. Roderick asked, who are you to tell me this? The woman said, I am from the Islands. She had been Shona's wet nurse but was banished as a witch many years earlier for warning her father that she had seen black crows circling the beach at Kyle and his body with them, soaring like an eagle. Later the Lord of the Isles took a force of young men to attack the farms on the mainland. It was a reprisal for a boat that had been stolen the year before. During the skirmish the lord was wounded, captured and thrown from a cliff. The fall broke his back. He lay on the beach three days and three nights before he died and the birds stripped the flesh from his bones. Roderick knew the story of the witch's prophecy and was enraged by her appearance at the feast, thinking she brought evil with her, and so ordered that she be taken at once and left on the road beyond the river. She told him, your brother has stolen the light from your eye, the blood from your veins, and this darkness you feel in your heart shall remain with you and your house forever. Roderick's love for his brother was as strong as his love for Shona. He tried to forget the woman's warning and yet a sadness filled him with a terrible longing for peace. The child grew and his likeness to Calum became unmistakable. Shona comforted Roderick and when she did so, lying in his arms, whispering his name, he knew the fear was of his own making. One day, six years after the birth of the child, he left the castle to make a journey to the western regions. At the head of the glen where the track crossed the watershed his horse stumbled and cut its foreleg. The wound was deep. Roderick bathed and bandaged it with a napkin and returned on foot, leading the animal. It was night. He stabled and fed the horse and lay down in the straw and fell asleep. When he awoke the sun was up. He left the stables and entered the castle. All was quiet. He climbed the stairs and found Shona and Calum together, the child sleeping between them. He dragged Calum from the bed and beat him senseless to the floor. He drew a dagger from his belt and gouged out his eyes. These he brought shiny and trembling to Shona. He carried the body into the courtyard and tied it to the back of the good grey stallion. He returned for the child. Shona pleaded with him for the life of her son. He held the knife to her breast, intending to kill her also, but her beauty was like the lily and her eyes as the clear sea. He took the child's hand and together they walked to where the horse stood in the courtyard. He held the boy close so that he would not see the body and they rode to the loch. He told the child to gather flowers from the shore. He carried Calum's body into the boat and covered it with his plaid. He called the boy and then rowed up the loch to where the waters roared under the cliff. As they neared the whirlpool he lowered Calum over the side. Although wounded and dying the water revived him and he gripped firm to the boat. Roderick gave the flowers to the boy and lifting him in his arms tossed him like a grain sack into the heart of Mathair Nan Uisgeachan. Calum heard the boy's screams and let go, his blind head turning towards the sound. The water sucked them down. It was done. Roderick forced the boat free and rowed back. When he returned and Shona learnt of her child's fate she cursed him and cried out for vengeance to the gods of her father, beat her fists against the wall until her knuckles bled and the bones in her fingers broke, and then she crawled on her knees through marsh stalks and mud to the shingle bank of the river where she laid her head under the water, and her body was like a swan on the white sands and fish played in the tresses of her hair. I turned my face to the rocks. I wept. I swam through seas thick with weed, diving and leaping in the sun. Only with strength could Mathair Nan Uisgeachan be conquered. I arrived at last on the shore and the shore was like a wild garden and the child picked flowers and when his arms were full came to where I was and gave them to me and I said, you have destroyed them, and flung the flowers down.

I opened my eyes. The room was changed.

'I had to wake you,' Aunt Magda said. 'It's almost lunch time.'

I lay in bed, floating back and forth, the vividness of the dream fierce within me. I had not moved. I was myself. Nothing had altered.

I washed and shaved. I dressed quickly. I felt the exhilaration of a man reprieved from death. I wanted to speak to Anne. I wanted to hear her voice. I went downstairs. The house was still and quiet, the drawing-room empty. I picked up the telephone. There was no answer from the castle and so I rang the office. Roger said that he had seen Anne earlier up at the loch.

'She's gone fishing,' he said. 'She took one of the children from the gypsy camp.'

RANDAL

She didn't blame Randal for leaving his. Day in, day out, boiled bacon. Sundays should be different. Sundays should be butcher's meat. But the world wasn't like that any more.

'I'm cold,' she said.

The clocks in the cottage were striking two. There was a grandfather clock in the front parlour and a marble clock on the mantelpiece in the kitchen where they sat eating. The grandfather clock had a strong steady tick, while the marble clock sounded fussy and overwound. Striking the hour, the grandfather clock sounded a stroke before the marble clock, so that the effect was of a slightly hysterical echo. It was as if the marble clock was repeating what the grandfather clock had just said, but distorting it in the process.

'Cold, cold,' said Madge.

Her sister Iseabal was staring at her. Her sister Iseabal had picked up the china teapot and was silently holding it out. She sat straightbacked in her straightbacked chair.

Madge coughed, then had to push her spectacles back to rest on the thin bridge of her nose. She lifted up her cup and saucer. Iseabal poured her a cup of tea. Madge did not take milk or sugar. She sipped the hot tea, but it scarcely warmed her.

'Those clocks are fast again,' said Iseabal.

Madge bit her lip. 'I put them right with my own hand,' she said.

'They're old,' said Iseabal. 'Listen to this one. It's got a hiccup in it.' She stirred three spoons of sugar into her tea. 'As for the grandfather,' she said, 'I think it's in its second childhood.'

The cottage kitchen was very small. There were three chairs at the kitchen table. Sitting there, you could reach out in any direction and almost touch a wall. All the walls were covered with the same rose-patterned wallpaper.

Madge reached out now and touched the marble clock affectionately. 'Remember Gregor MacGregor?' she said.

Iseabal sighed. 'What should I want to remember him for?'

'Gregor MacGregor was wicked,' Madge said, stroking the face of the marble clock. 'He carried hay on a Sunday. Drunk as a faucet he was, most of the time. And when he wasn't drunk he was hogging.' Her plump round cheeks dimpled above a sentimental smile. 'He'd promise you anything,' she went on, 'but you'd never get it. He'd promise you the sea, he would; he'd promise you the sea, and the mountain. Anything that wasn't his to give. His promise was like the froth on the water. And cunning. "The fox knows well, where the geese dwell!" He wouldn't just steal your eggs. Or your hen. Not Gregor MacGregor. Ambitious, he was. Steal your eggs *and* your hen. That was Gregor.'

Her sister Iseabal was making her fingers crack by clasping her bony hands together. Madge acknowledged by the merest pause the unease which this noise betokened. Then she went on:

'Steal eggs and hen and tip his cap and tell you he was doing you a favour. What good it ever did him I don't know. If you ask me he was more than half-daft. Never satisfied, Gregor MacGregor. In winter it was August, August, August he'd be talking of. In summer he was all for Christmas. You never know where you are with a man like that.'

Iseabal sniffed, and brushed back a wisp of her iron-grey hair. 'A pity he never used his teeth to stop his tongue,' she said.

There were three plates on the kitchen table. Two of the plates on the kitchen table were empty. Madge shivered and coughed and pushed her empty plate aside with a trembling thumb. Then she stood up and went to the little window over the sink.

'Remember when Parlan caught him out over the white goat?' she said. 'He was that angry, Parlan, he hit him with a big stick, and Gregor fell in the cesspit.' She chuckled to herself at the memory. 'So Gregor takes a chicken in a sack,' she murmured, watching her breath cloud the cold window pane, 'and he climbs up on Parlan's roof and drops that chicken down the chimney just when Parlan's daughter had the plum jam stewing on the fire. A chicken squawking round the kitchen all covered in hot plum jam! It took them weeks to scrub it off the ceiling. And, as if that wasn't sufficient, Gregor went and wrote a poem about Parlan and every verse ending with "I trust he finds thorns in his porridge", and the funny thing was, when Parlan read the poem—'

'That's enough,' said Iseabal sharply. 'I don't want to hear another word about Gregor MacGregor. He's dead.'

The word hung in the thin air of the kitchen like an icicle.

'Quick to the feast,' said Madge, 'quick to the grave.'

Iseabal was making her fingers crack again. 'He was dead before he died,' she said. 'Dead, who is not in God. Dead then. Dead now.'

Madge pressed her lips lightly to the cold glass. 'He was so small,' she said.

Iseabal stood up from the table and pushed back her chair. 'We'll have that nice bath after we've washed up,' Iseabal said. 'A proper Sunday bath.'

'I'm cold,' said Madge. She coughed. 'Remember the bad winter?' she said. 'When all the swedes and mangolds got frozen and Randal ran out of hay after the summer being so wet, and the sheep were dying and their fleeces all stiff and stuck to the ground, and some of them with their legs broken, coming into the house for a bit of potato peelings, anything, and then the snow so deep it was high over the hedge there.'

Iseabal leaned on her outspread fingers. The nails showed purple with the weight, but the tips were white. 'That bath,' she said. 'Do you hear me?'

'I hear you,' Madge said. She did not turn away from the window. Her forehead was resting against the pane. 'I was here in the kitchen washing up,' she said, 'and the egg wouldn't come off the eggcups no matter how hot the water, and me scratching away with the scourer, it just wouldn't come off, and I heard this bleating, and I had to scrape the ice off the catch before I could get the window open, and the glass itself all over coated with frost so you couldn't see through it. And when I got the window open, there was this lamb by the drain, and the drain frozen solid, and the lamb bleating and bleating, just born, not long born, the night before perhaps it was, and it was all red and wet and smudgy one side of its head.' She turned away from the window and faced her sister Iseabal. 'A crow had picked its eye out,' she said.

The sisters looked at each other calmly for a moment. Then:

'That's enough,' said Iseabal. 'We'll wash up first.'

Madge nodded and went back to the table and put her cup and saucer on her plate. She reached across and gathered up the others. She said, 'Can't say I blame Randal for leaving that boiled bacon. Too salty.'

'A matter of taste,' said Iseabal.

Carrying the cups and plates towards the sink, Madge stopped to look out of the window again. 'It's snowing,' she said, in a cheerful voice.

Her sister was just behind her. 'Nice,' her sister was saying. 'Like those streaks in Randal's hair.'

Madge watched the snow stream and make brief flowers on the pane. She coughed. 'It was red as fire once,' she said. She put the plates and cups and knives and forks into the low sink. Her sister had taken the black pan of water from the grate and now it was being held out towards her with the long handle wrapped in Iseabal's apron. Madge poured the water into the sink and rolled the sleeves of her dress and started washing up.

'Did you say red?' said Iseabal.

'No,' Madge said.

'Did you say Randal's hair was *red*?'

'No,' Madge said.

'You did,' said her sister.

'I didn't,' Madge said. 'Are you going to dry?'

'Red, you said.'

'Black,' Madge said, looking at her hands working in the water. 'Black.'

'Yes, but you said red,' said Iseabal. 'You said it was red.'

Madge scrubbed at the bacon marks with a piece of wire wool. 'Look,' she said, 'what are we arguing for? I know the colour of my brother's hair.'

'I should think so,' said Iseabal. 'Black.'

'As the crow,' Madge said.

The cat purred on the hearth.

Iseabal polished the plates fiercely with a thin cloth. 'A streak of white about the temples makes a man distinguished,' Iseabal said. 'But it wouldn't if his hair was red.'

'No,' said Madge.

'Never trust a man with red hair,' her sister said. 'Black hair is straightforward hair. Randal's hair is good black.'

'I know it,' said Madge wearily. 'Didn't I say so? Don't I keep on saying so?'

Iseabal smiled at her own reflection in a spoon. Then she turned aside to hang up their cups on the hooks in the dresser.

'What can Randal be thinking of you?' Iseabal said softly.

Madge did not look at her. Instead, she turned right round and said in a bold voice, 'What *do* you think of me, Randal?'

Iseabal reached out her finger and made a cup swing. The marble clock ticked fussily. Iseabal nodded her head.

'What did he say?' Madge asked at last.

Iseabal smiled. 'You heard him,' she said.

'I didn't quite catch it.'

'What's the matter with you,' said Iseabal, 'that you don't hear your own flesh and blood when he speaks to you?'

Madge pushed her glasses up her nose. She said nothing. She returned her attention to the sink.

'Ashamed of her?' said Iseabal. 'Yes, I am too.'

Madge poked at the crockery in the water. 'He didn't say that,' she said. Her voice was a whisper.

'That's what he said,' said Iseabal.

'I don't believe it,' Madge muttered.

Iseabal shrugged, putting away the knives. 'You have little faith,' she said.

'No,' said Madge savagely. 'He didn't say that. He didn't.' Iseabal wiped her fingers on the towel that hung from a nail beside the sink. 'He speaks his mind straight,' she said, and sniffed.

Madge pulled out the plug. The water ran away with a choking sound.

'I'll get the bath in from the outhouse,' Madge said, in a voice that sought to please two people.

'Fine,' her sister said. 'You go ahead, dear.'

Madge slipped on her coat and went out of the door. The snow was flying up the hill. The sky looked like a bad egg, full of it. She pulled up her collar and hurried across the yard. The tin bath made a jagged black mark, revealing the gravel under the snow, as she dragged it back to the cottage from the outhouse.

Madge came in coughing with the cold. 'Give me a hand,' she said. 'You know it's heavy.'

She had her back towards her sister, dragging the bath, so she could not see what was happening in the room.

When Madge turned round she saw that her sister had her finger to her lips. Iseabal was kneeling in front of the easy chair. 'Randal's fallen asleep,' she whispered.

'So I see,' said Madge.

'Well,' she went on, after a moment's silence, 'shall I fetch it?'

'No,' Iseabal said, 'I will,' and she went out smiling, on tip-toes.

Madge pulled the curtains shut as softly as she could. The little rings made a rushing noise. She looked round nervously. The light from the grate was almost golden with the curtains drawn.

The cat twitched in a bad dream, or as its heart missed a beat.

Madge slipped off her coat and dragged the bath in front of the fire without making a sound. Then she picked up the

scuttle in her arms, and set it down beside the bath. She
knelt. She took sticks and papers and pieces of coal
from the scuttle and began arranging them inside the bath.
She worked neatly, making a pattern.

Her sister Iseabal came back in with snow across her hair.
She carried a green can in each hand.

'There,' Iseabal said, putting the cans down beside the
bath. 'Good. You put the sticks and papers in.'

'And some bits of coal,' Madge said.

Iseabal smiled. 'Isn't that a waste?'

'You never know,' Madge said.

Her sister shrugged, accepting, and unscrewed the top of
one of the green cans. She poured a thin stream into the
bath.

'More than that,' Madge said.

'It's plenty,' said Iseabal.

'Let me do it,' Madge said, standing up.

She took the can from her sister and walked right round
the bath, pouring freely as she went. When she reached the
spot where she had started, she stopped, nodded to her
sister, and went round once more, still pouring.

'That will do,' Iseabal said.

'Yes,' said Madge. 'That will do.'

She set down the empty can and they stood looking at
each other. Iseabal shook the snow from her grey hair with an
almost flirtatious gesture, and smiled. Iseabal's fingers came
up to touch the smile on her own face as if to make sure it
was there. After that they avoided each other's eyes.

Madge undressed quickly. Half-turned away from the
chair, she held out her hand and her sister took it. Iseabal's
hand was hot. Madge helped her sister into the bath. Iseabal
knelt down.

'Go on,' Iseabal said.

Madge picked up the other green can and unscrewed the
top. She poured half of the contents over her sister without
looking at her. She could hear it trickling down.

'It's stinky,' Iseabal said.

'Well,' said Madge, 'what do you expect it to be?'

'I'm not complaining,' said Iseabal.

Madge nodded. She climbed into the bath and handed her sister the can. She knelt down facing Iseabal, but with her glasses off and her eyes shut. She felt the liquid pouring over her.

Madge tilted up her face. 'Plenty in my hair,' she said, and some ran into her mouth.

Madge coughed.

'Sorry,' said her sister.

'Never mind,' said Madge.

In the dark, with her eyes tight shut, Madge could hear the marble clock ticking. She waited. 'Go on then,' she said at last.

'I thought you had them,' Iseabal said.

Madge opened her eyes. For the first time since taking off their clothes, they looked at each other. Iseabal was smiling. 'There's a box in the knife drawer,' Iseabal said. 'Or we could use a taper.'

'That would not be right,' Madge said. She climbed out of the bath, groped around on the floor until she found her glasses, put them on, and went to the dresser. The matchbox was wrapped in a table napkin, beside the cheese grater. Madge unfolded the napkin and put the matchbox on the table. She refolded the napkin and replaced it in the drawer. Then she shut the drawer. She picked up the matchbox from the table and went back to the bath.

Madge removed her spectacles and knelt down once more facing her sister. She clasped the matchbox in her right hand. Its edge was sharp against her palm.

'Randal's still asleep,' said Iseabal.

'Of course,' said Madge.

She looked into her sister's eyes but she could only see herself reflected there. The firelight flickered across Iseabal's proud face.

'Shall I say a prayer?' Madge asked.

'Can you remember one?' said her sister.

'No,' Madge admitted. 'I can't.'

The two clocks struck the half hour, with the grandfather as usual a heart-beat in front.

'The devil,' said Iseabal.

'Never mind,' Madge said.

The fire crackled in the grate.

'Mercy on us,' said Iseabal.

'Amen,' Madge said.

The cat looked up at them with bright unwondering eyes, then put its head back between its black and white paws.

'I never did like that graveyard,' said Iseabal.

Madge nodded absent-mindedly, giving her sister the box of matches into her hand. Then she said, as an afterthought, catching at Iseabal's wrist, 'But I don't think *you* should strike the match.'

'Why not?' said Iseabal.

'I just don't think you should,' Madge said.

Iseabal smiled. 'All right,' she said. 'You do it. You and your remembering. But you were always the strong one, really.'

'No doubt,' said Madge. 'But I don't think I should do it either.'

Iseabal smiled. 'Who then?' she said.

'Who?' said Madge. 'You know who.'

'Randal,' said Iseabal softly.

'Randal,' Madge said in a great voice.

They both shut their eyes. There came the sound of the striking of a match against the matchbox. At first it would not light. The match had to scrape against the box twice without success. The third time it lit.

THE BROTHERS

First of all, I should like to say that I don't believe in ghosts, and yet some strange things have been happening to me recently. And you won't understand them unless I tell you something about myself. I am a writer, and I was born and brought up in the Highlands of Scotland where, I may tell you, you can hear plenty of ghost stories. For instance, there was the man who used to get up from the ceilidh in the middle of the night and who would come back much later, his shoes and trousers dripping: he had been carrying the coffin of someone who had not yet died and who perhaps was telling a story at that very ceilidh. Imagine what it must have been like to be such a man. Anyway, I myself don't believe in these stories, though I have heard them often. My father told me once that he nearly turned back one night when passing a cemetery after seeing a green light there, but he carried on, and found that it was the phosphorescence from fish lying in a cart which had been put in the ditch by the drunken driver. I believe that, but I don't believe in ghosts.

However, let me say that when I was old enough I left the Highlands and came to Edinburgh and began to write stories and novels in English. I left the Gaelic world wholly behind me, because I suppose I despised it. If you ask me why I despise it it is partly because of these silly ghost stories and partly because of the simple unsophisticated mode of life of those people whom I have little affection for. In fact when I was growing up they seemed to laugh at me. I have even written articles attacking that placid unchanging world which knows nothing of Kafka or Proust or the other great writers of the world. I would never go back there now, so I live in my untidy flat in Edinburgh seeing very few people and working at my books, some of which have been published. I have set none of them, I may say, in the Highlands. After all, what important insight could I get from there, from people and a culture which have not moved into the twentieth century?

All was going well until recently when one night working on a book about Joseph and his brothers – after all, I don't see why Thomas Mann should be the only person who is allowed to write about the Bible – I came down to the living-room where I had left my typewriter. I remembered quite clearly at which point I had stopped writing. Joseph was standing in astonishment gazing at the pyramids and comparing them to the hills of home, and, exiled in a strange land, feeling very small against that hewn stone. The moonlight was shining on my typewriter and making it look like a yellow skeleton against the window. I switched on the light and picked up the pages which were still in the typewriter. I began to read them, remembering in my mind, insomniac and restless, the cadences which I had aimed for and which I thought I had achieved. However, with an astonishment as great as Joseph's when he was regarding the pyramids, I suddenly found that I was reading Gaelic.

Now there is absolutely no question but that these pages had been written in English. I had spent too long over the words not to know that. However, as I read these Gaelic sentences, rougher and more passionate than my English ones, I had a strange feeling that I had read them before somewhere. I stood there astonished in the silence. There was no sound in any of the other flats or on the street outside. I looked carefully round my now brightly-lit room but it seemed exactly the same as when I had gone to bed. My Penguins were arranged carefully round the walls, and my typewriter was on the table. I stared at the pages knowing that I must be going out of my mind. But I was absolutely certain that though these pages were familiar I had not written them. They seemed to be saying in Gaelic that Joseph had abandoned his land for another land and that in doing so he had betrayed his own. Someone must have typed these pages but who could that someone have been?

No living human being could have entered the flat and

certainly no one could have typed the pages without my hearing them. On the other hand, no one could have typed them and brought them into the flat as a practical joke. I am very fearful and I lock the windows, and the door is always locked. But not only that, my English pages had disappeared. Whoever had done this had not simply translated the original pages, but had rather substituted his Gaelic pages for my English ones. And yet since that person was not me it must have been some spiritual being, in other words a ghost. I felt for the first time a draught as of cold air all round me even in the bright electric light. I went to the door but it was still locked. I switched on all the lights in every room but they were undisturbed and the windows were all locked as I had left them.

I came back to the room and stood looking down at the Gaelic pages. They were even written on the same kind of quarto paper as I had used myself and the typing was not unlike mine. But it was slightly different, the touch was lighter and surer. There were fewer erasures. The cold wind did not go away. I felt threatened as if some being whose name and form I did not know understood all about me and was determined to destroy me.

I made coffee and stayed up all night, I was too frightened to go to bed. I went and got my red and green dressing-gown and sat by the electric fire, though I could ill-afford to waste all that electricity. But there was nothing else that I could do. I listened to the silence, terrified that that ghostly being would return and type while I sat there. What was I going to do? Carefully I put the case back on the type-writer and stared at it as if hypnotized. I was afraid that I would fall asleep and that the ghost would type more while I sat transfixed there like a mummy. But nothing happened and when morning dawned sickly and pale I looked again at the pages. They were still in Gaelic. My English ones had irretrievably disappeared.

The following day I summoned up enough courage to burn the Gaelic pages and start again on my English version. I retyped as far as I could remember what I had already done and went on to describe the sophisticated world of Egypt. I knew little about the country but imagined the kind of civilization that would have produced those vast inhuman monuments. I invented a slave market at which Joseph was sold, I wrote about himself and Potiphar's wife. I may say that I had difficulty here since my sexual experiences have been limited and I know whom to blame for that. At five o'clock, satisfied with my work, I made some coffee and at that moment I heard it.

The sound was coming from the next room where I keep my record player. It was the voice of a well-known Gaelic singer and she was singing a song about the murder of a younger brother by an older one. I rushed into the room, spilling my coffee as I went. There was the record player plugged in and there was the record which I'd never seen in my life spinning on its black circuit. I switched the machine off and removed the record. Though I had never seen it, I had of course understood the words. I passed my hand across my brow and put the record down on the floor. I closed the cover of the record player and sat there dismally in the dull afternoon whose light was already fading from the sky. I didn't know what to do. I could have gone out to see a film or a play but I didn't fancy coming back to my flat in the middle of the night. I switched on all the lights again. I heard no one moving about the room. My jazz and classical records were still in their places. I trembled with fear and anguish.

Suddenly I rushed back into the room where I had left my latest English pages. I picked them up. They were all in Gaelic and without erasure. I read them with horror. They said that Joseph had been condemned to death and was lying in prison waiting for the end. This too, of course, was in the story. After all, it is one of the great stories of the world. My mother had told it to me many years before in a voice of rigour and appalling judgment. But since then I had read Thomas Mann.

I saw him quite clearly sitting in prison, the light about him dim and grey and his face quite blank. It was as if he was a white page waiting to be written on. All around him was Egypt which he had learned to love and whose language he spoke. I saw the walls of the prison and written on them were graffiti in a language which might have been Egyptian since they did not appear to be composed of any language that I had ever seen. He was dressed in his coat of many colours.

I sat dully at the typewriter with these pages in my hand. They were strong, powerful pages, in fact better than mine, simpler and perhaps cruder. It's difficult to explain why they were so much better, but I think it must have been because their language was less abstract. They seemed to have caught the intonation of a language that Joseph might have used, perhaps Hebrew, perhaps Egyptian. They even incorporated the words of the song I had heard on the record player. If I had had somewhere to go I would have rushed out that moment on to the street. But I had no friends in Edinburgh. Its vast stony houses were anonymous enough for me to be able to write among them in privacy, but they were not places for friendship. I stared at the light draining out of the sky and I was more frightened than I had ever been in my whole life, or rather I was frightened in a different way from that in which I had been frightened before. I felt like a statue which was also trembling. I made more coffee and kept all the lights on but I was on edge, as if waiting for a fresh incursion into my life which I had thought ordered. I waited there helplessly, as a cow waits to be pole-axed. I remembered seeing that once back in the Highlands and I had hated it. Now I was the victim myself in all that bright light. I knew I would have to stay up again all night. I would be frightened to lie in my bed among the cold stiff blankets, waiting for the dawn to appear. And as I waited I knew that some spirit was moving about me, determined to destroy me. I put the last page of the Gaelic script in the typewriter as if I was propitiating an angry god. And I sat there like that for a long time, shivering though the fire was warm.

It must have been about seven o'clock at night that I sud-

denly felt a terrible anger with whatever malevolent being
was about me. The curtains were drawn, the electric fire was
on, there was lots of light. Suddenly I took the Gaelic pages
out of the typewriter, screwed them up and threw them into
the wastepaper basket. I knew exactly why I had done this.
I knew that I must not surrender at this point or I would
surrender forever. Why should I allow this being, whatever
it was, to tell me what I ought to do, how I ought to write?
I was only doing what I thought I ought to be doing. Did I
not have free will? What law stated that some ghost or other
from another world should command my mind? The anger
I felt was pure and ardent and innocent. If I wished to
abandon my homeland, if that was what I was doing, why
should I not do so? Indeed, in doing so was I not being an
exception? Was I not in fact setting out to create a new
being? That is, the exile who is able to speak from another
land and in another language? I had been betrayed by my
own land. What therefore did I owe it? I too had been
mocked by my own brothers, if I could call them that. Well
then, let me stay in my Egypt. Let me adopt it as my promised land. Let my ambitions be fructified there. After all,
wasn't Egypt the pinnacle of achievement? And in Egypt
could I not gather my corn together and feed my rustic
brothers who came down there from my own lost land?
What was wrong with that? Wasn't that what the Joseph
story taught, that the murderous brothers were dependent
after all on the dreamer who lived in another and more
powerful country?

So, out of my pure anger, I tore the Gaelic pages out of
the typewriter and threw them into the wastepaper basket.
And I waited. That's precisely what I did. I waited. I knew
that something would happen though I did not know what
it would be. I was frightened, yes, but I was angry too and
the clean wash of my anger anaesthetized for a while my
fear, at least as long as I could hear people passing on the
street in my adopted city. I listened to those feet passing and
I felt in my own country. I even summoned up enough
strength to start typing again in English. I wrote how Joseph

left the prison because he was able to interpret the dreams of the baker and the butler. I thought of myself as Joseph, the dreamer who had such great powers.

And the night passed and became more silent. Once I had to leave the room where my typewriter was and go to the bathroom. For a second, as I opened the door, I thought I saw a figure in white flashing past me, but I decided that it probably was an illusion. It seemed to me that the figure was dressed in a white robe which had an oriental look about it. But, as I have said, I decided that it must have been an illusion. Not an illusion however was the intense cold I felt as I left the room and all the time I was in the bathroom. And worse was when leaving the bathroom I looked in the mirror and saw my own face there. It seemed demonic and lined and white. I could hardly recognize myself. It was as if I was waiting for something to happen, something devilish and horrifying. I went back to the room, trembling again, and when I did so I saw that the pages in the typewriter were written once more in Gaelic.

I withdrew my eyes from the pages as if afraid that they contained sentences which would destroy me. My English pages had again disappeared. I looked down at my hands, wondering perhaps if I myself was the author of what was happening to me. But I could learn nothing from them. They looked innocent and bland. I looked at the clock. It said eleven. The noises in the street seemed to have stopped and there was an oppressive air of waiting about the flat. I went right through it and checked that every light was switched on. I waited as if listening for songs but I heard nothing. I went back and sat down again in my chair which seemed to have turned into a gaunt throne. Was I indeed Joseph, sitting in that alien chair? The wood on which I sat seemed to be rotting as if small animals were eating into it. There were the marks of teeth. I saw in my mind cows eating each other, cornstacks devouring one another. I was afloat on the river of time. I can't tell the visions I saw that night. It was as if I was in the centre of Egypt and there were snakes and cats all round me. They opened their mouths, and their teeth and

fangs snapped at me. The throne or chair tottered. The
furniture swayed. The pages seemed to turn into tablets,
solid and white.

Suddenly I thought, what if the story of Joseph could
have a different ending? And I was terrified. After all, I
hadn't believed in the Bible, or had thought of it only as
fiction. Well, if it were fiction, then alternatives were possible. Who was this Joseph anyway but an arrogant fellow who
thought that he was better than his brothers? Wasn't that
the case? Weren't the brothers justified in getting rid of him?
I hadn't thought of that before, and yet wasn't that what the
Gaelic typed pages had been telling me? If that were so,
then the Joseph story could be turned inside out. Joseph had
deserved everything he had got. He had deserved his Egypt.
I imagined outside my room the tall stone buildings as if
they were pyramids. Inside them were all the buried kings,
the tyrants and despots. He had joined them. He had taken
his robe down to Egypt and seen it encrusted with gold before his eyes. He had entered that alien time and place.

I sat trembling. After a very long time I brought myself to
look at the Gaelic pages. They said in prose stronger than
my English:

Joseph was a traitor. His journey was arrogant and aristocratic. We brothers believe that he betrayed us, that he
hated our language and our way of life. We speak for the
oppressed and inarticulate countrymen who live in the
small places far from the city. We come to see him not
because we wish to eat his corn but rather because we
wish to destroy him utterly. He hated us, therefore we
must hate him.

I listened and as I listened it was as if the whole flat came
alive with sounds. These sounds it is difficult to describe.
Partly they were of music that I thought I had forgotten,
fragments of songs about sailing ships and men exiled from
their own land. Partly they were the sounds of cows mooing
on early, almost forgotten moors. Partly they were the
sounds of human voices at street corners. Partly they were

voices telling stories. Partly they were my own voice heard so long ago. And the night darkened and lengthened. The curtains shivered in the draught. My mind was a mosaic of different sentences, some in English, some in Gaelic. My whole body was sweating as if with an incurable fever. I remember getting up and for no reason shifting the position of the green-faced clock on the mantelpiece. There was a dreadful coldness all around me, though the two bars of the electric fire were on. I looked at the telephone as if it were a snake about to strike. For some reason or other I thought of all the family photographs I had destroyed.

And I sat on my throne in the middle of the night. And as I sat there listening to the sound of feet on the road I clearly heard steps which seemed much more purposeful than the ones I had heard earlier on. I can't describe why I felt this. It was something to do with the fact that the sounds made by the feet seemed to reinforce each other as if three people were walking along together, and as if they were making for a predetermined rendezvous. But at the same time the sound seemed curiously alien and echoing. The footsteps were purposeful and foreign and hollow, and they were, I was sure, making for my door. In a sudden panic I arose from my chair and pulled the bolt across the outer door, which was already locked. I don't know why I did this since I knew that locks and bolts would not keep these beings, familiar and fatal, out. But I did it anyway and went back to my room and shut that door as well. I waited by the fire, shivering. I was alone and afraid. There was no question of that.

When I happened at that moment to glance at the pages still in the typewriter, the machine began to move of its own accord. I may say at this point that I had been so terrified by all the things that had happened that I almost accepted this strange event. I had once seen a teleprinter almost supernaturally receiving messages from a different place, miles and miles away, and as I accepted that so I accepted this. The typewriter was writing in capital letters WE ARE COMING FOR YOU JOSEPH WE ARE COMING TO TAKE YOU HOME. I cannot describe the menace that these simple words seemed to contain. What did HOME mean? The grave? The words leapt out at me in their large threatening capitals. They seemed to emanate from a different world, one far from mine.

And simultaneously I heard drunken voices coming from behind my door. The drunken discordant voices were singing a Gaelic song or what seemed to be one. I can't wholly describe that song. It was, I thought, Gaelic and yet there were cadences in it of another country, an oriental country. I could almost have thought that the cadences might have been Egyptian. They were aureate and intricate and yet below them I could hear quite clearly the words of the Gaelic song, just as I had heard them many years before in my own home. It was a Gaelic song and yet the words seemed to come not through mouths but rather through snouts. I imagined at the door, just outside, three snouts raised to the moon. At the same time I sensed a menace such as one might feel – not from an animal but from a being other than animal or man, a being from another world, a world that existed long ago with its irrational gods and stiff hieratic clothes.

I stared at the door which was painted a bright yellow. My room is painted in two colours: two walls are black, the other two are yellow. When I looked at the yellow door it was as if I was looking at a screen that divided me from another world. It was as if the door was not made of wood but of a fine delicate skin which blazed with the power of the sun. And it was a skin that I knew would not survive if those beings, alive and barbarous and drunken, were to decide to burst through it. Their song was a lament and a song of triumph. It was menacing and despairing and fruitful. Suddenly, as I looked, words began to appear on the door, some in Gaelic and some in English and some in a strange language that I did not know. It was like the writing on the wall that had appeared to Belshazzar.

There was then for a while silence. The drunken voices ceased. I knew that they were giving me time, and I did not know what I was going to do with that time they had given me. They had come down from their hills and they were waiting for me to act. They were waiting for a gesture from me. What would that gesture be? For I knew that these were not my real brothers, not the brothers I had been brought up with, not the brothers whose toys I had shared or smashed, not the brothers with whom I had bedded in that cramped house so long ago. These were other brothers. And their song was a menacing song.

I looked down at my clothes and found, to my surprise, that I was wearing not my cloak of many colours but a coat of pure yellow, the colour of the door. If I wanted to save myself I knew what I must do. Did I want to save myself? And was it only an instinct for self-protection that drove me to my action? That in itself would not be enough. No, it wasn't wholly that, perhaps not that at all. It wasn't just that, for as I listened I heard the Gaelic tune again, and my blood seemed to move with it, warmly and purely. I walked slowly to the door but it was as if I were dancing. A strange perfume seemed to fill the entire room. It wasn't however the perfume of the east, it was a more local perfume, such as I had often smelt so long ago. It was the perfume perhaps of heatherbells, of brine. It was harsh and pure and severe and it suffused my whole body. It was a perfume that I seemed almost to remember.

As I moved towards the door the words on it changed their shape and became not fragmentary but wholly Gaelic. I knew that outside the door my brothers were waiting. I knew that I must welcome them not with hauteur but with deference. I must not be the successful Egyptian but the humbled Hebrew. I knew that it was I who was the sinner. My eyes pierced the door which was like skin and on the other side I saw my brothers broken by defeat and starvation but still human and rustic and brave. It was to them that I must offer myself, not to the alien kings and an alien land. It was to them that I must, if necessary, be the sacrifice. In the silence of the night which trembled with so many stars I walked towards the door and felt my body gain energy and power. It was as if I was a king, a real king, because I had ceased to think like one. I reached the door. It had ceased to be skin and was wood again. I opened it but there was no one there.

I looked around me. The typewriter sat on its own in the moonlight. I sat down at it in the peaceful night and began to type. The words were Gaelic and flowed easily and familiarly, as if I were speaking to my brothers who had sung drunken songs outside my door. I looked down at my clothes and found that they were all one colour. I dreamed as I wrote and my dream was reflected easily in my words. I seemed to see faces, worn and lined, and they were more beautiful than any other faces I had known. I seemed to hear their language and it was their language that I wrote. It was rough and yet it was my own. It was their voices speaking through me, maimed and triumphant and without sophistication. I seemed to see the moonlight shining on the corn, ripe and yellow, the colour of the door. To their starving faces I brought joy as I wrote. And inside me was their song. I sat in my yellow robe at my yellow typewriter in the yellow room. And I was happy. I overflowed with the most holy joy.

PROUD LADY IN A CAGE

'Here, hen, are ye sleepin'?'

The voice came from among the women skirling and shouting obscenities around the cage, laughing lewdly and gloating over the prisoner's humiliation. It came from a small wizened-faced witch who had joukit past the English guards and was rattling the iron bars. The prisoner stood erect and looked disdainfully over the harridan's head. But she could not ignore her. The leering face grew larger and larger, blotting out the other women; the rattling got louder and the voice shriller, drowning the screams and the jeers.

'I cannie stand here all day till you come out o' yer daydreams, hen. I asked a civil question, and I want a civil answer.'

Bella Logan came back through the whirling currents of centuries until her eyes focused on the woman's face. She shook her head to clear away the nightmare. She was aware again of the intense cold, and her teeth chattered.

'Are ye all right, hen?' the little woman said, peering inquisitively with bird-bright eyes through the glass and thin gilt bars encircling the enquiry desk. Bella recognized her as Mrs Cessford, who lived in a vennel on the banks of the Tweed with her grandson, Zander, a tall skeleton-thin lad with long carroty hair who did odd jobs in the supermarket.

'Ye look as if ye'd seen a ghost, hen.'

'I'm okay,' Bella whispered. 'I think.'

She closed her eyes for a moment and saw again the crowd of harpies and the great iron bars of the cage. Her neck was still raw from the rope that had been around it.

'Is it yer monthly, hen?' Mrs Cessford leered sympathetically. 'Oh, I ken what it is!'

Bella nodded. It was a lie. But better to pretend to this old bitch than have her blazoning the truth abroad. Not that anybody would believe what had been happening to

her. The cold terror of it drooped over her like a frozen
shroud.

'I was wantin' the shredded wheat, hen,' Mrs Cessford
said. 'I've been huntin' everywhere but I cannie find it.
Where have they put it? Or are ye no' sellin' such simple
things as shredded wheat in this braw new place? I cannie
see why ye needed to move. The auld store in the Wool
Market was guid enough for me and folk like me. I don't
think I'll ever get used to this great barn o' a place.'

Bella held her throat with one hand as she directed Mrs
Cessford to Aisle Seven where the cereals and their assorted
companions were shelved. 'Ta, hen!' Mrs Cessford leered
and set off, her shopping bag and the supermarket's wire-
basket slapping against her spindly shanks on either side.
'You watch that period now, and I'll dance at yer weddin'.'

Bella shivered. The enquiry desk that stood on a raised
dais in the middle of the new supermarket had felt like a
refrigerator ever since she set foot in it this morning, just
before the store opened for the first time. She was in the
cash desk of the old store, and while this new building near
the railway station was going up Mr Stott, the manager,
had offered her promotion, asking her to take charge of the
enquiry desk the owners thought necessary in the new supermarket's vastness. 'Our public is sure to get lost and need a
helping hand, Miss Logan,' Mr Stott had simpered. Bella
experienced a pleasant glow of satisfaction, thinking of the
rise in salary, when she entered it for the first time. But the
glow had been dispelled by the sudden unearthly chill that
had crept through her limbs. And then *that* had happened.

Despite the darts of icy cold that still pierced every part
of her, her neck burned. It was a great red-hot itch. She
closed her eyes and massaged it with her fingertips. Then
she felt herself being drawn back into the nightmare. Once
again the rope was almost choking her. Once again she could
see the great backside of the horse she'd been dragged behind, her hands tied at her back. The soldier on the horse
had turned round every now and then, laughing and jeering
at her as he jerked the rope to make her stumble. And the

watching crowd laughed with him, shouting: 'Come 'n' see
the prood leddy bein' draggit through the mire! Come 'n'
see braw Bella o' Buchan drinkin' in the reek frae the
horse's dock!'

They had come to an iron cage suspended by chains from
the castle's battlements. The cage was about six feet high
and three feet in diameter. It swung a yard and a half above
the ground. The rope was taken from her neck, her hands
were untied; then two soldiers lifted her and flung her so
violently through the door of the cage that she fell, banging
her forehead against the bars. She was raising herself on her
knees when the door clanged. A herald started a proclam-
ation, but she could hear nothing until he came to the
words: '. . . be incarcerated here in his burgh of Berwick-on-
Tweed during His Majesty's pleasure. And may God have
mercy on her and cause her to repent and plead for the
mercy of His Majesty.'

'Never!' she cried, standing straight in the narrow cage
and looking disdainfully over the heads of the crowd.

It was then that the harpies had surged forward, surrounding the cage and cackling obscenely.

Bella lifted her handbag from the floor beside her feet and
took out a small mirror. Looking to make sure nobody was
watching, she held the mirror to her neck. There was a
broad red weal around it.

She shivered with cold and dread. Had she fallen asleep,
and was it a nightmare? But she knew she hadn't slept. And
the livid weal was not out of a dream.

Bella Logan was totally lacking in imagination. She knew
nothing of history or tradition; she was prosaic and un-
romantic. She never read a book. Every week she bought
two or three women's magazines but never read anything in
them except the knitting patterns. She knitted constantly. In
the cash desk in the old store she had always had a partly
knitted jumper or pullover, scarf or socks on her knee,
knitting needles clicking quickly between customers. A part-
finished magenta cardigan was in the pink-and-fawn striped

knitting bag lying at her feet this morning, but she hadn't managed to take it out yet. She never made mistakes with her additions on the cash-register, never dropped a stitch or made miscalculations with her knitting. In the Kelpie, the pub seven miles from Berwick that she visited on Saturday nights with Rod Wishart, she chalked the scores of the darts team on the blackboard, and never once had anybody found her making a mistake. She did the mental arithmetic easily, automatically, and was usually talking to somebody while doing it.

Bella was twenty-two. She was an only child, lived with her parents and was dominated by her mother. Mrs Logan, in her turn, was dominated by her mother, Mrs Dickie, a formidable eighty-three-year-old. Mrs Dickie's name was Isabella, though she'd always been called Bella. She had christened her daughter Isabella too, but Isa Logan had insisted on being called Isa since she was four years old; she would never, on any account, answer to 'Bella'. Yet when she christened her own daughter Isabella, she decreed that the child was to be called 'Bella' from the start. 'After your granny, dear. You love your granny, don't you? So what could be better than being called after her? We can't have two Isas in the house. It would be a fine how-d'ye-do and cause no end of trouble. So Bella you're going to be, my girl. And like it.'

Bella Logan never protested. She accepted the name as phlegmatically as she accepted everything else. When rude boys at school used to shout, 'Let me rub yer belly, Bella!' she had always tossed her head and sniffed. Once, after he had been to Sicily for ten days' holiday, Rod Wishart had said: 'Bella! It means beautiful in Italian. Bella bellissima!'

'So what?' Bella said.

She had been walking out with Rod Wishart for three years. They had never had sexual relations, though often Rod's need had been urgent when they were walking over the golf links in the dark or when they'd been coming home in his firm's car after drinking at the Kelpie. But Bella would never do anything to ease him. 'I'm not going to do it till

we're married,' she said. 'I respect myself if you don't, Rod
Wishart. My mother would have fifty fits if she knew what
you keep trying to do.'

'Well, let's get married then,' he always replied. 'What're
we waiting for?'

'I'm not going to get married till I'm twenty-five. I don't
see why I should tie myself down.'

'What about me?' he said. 'I can't go on like this. I want
us to get settled down and . . . and, well, I suppose we should
have some bairns . . .'

'I don't want to be a mother just yet,' she said primly.
'Besides, you keep saying your firm might shift you to another territory. We'd better wait till that gets settled.'

Rod was the representative for a company that sold agri-
cultural foods and seeds to farmers. He spent most of his
life in the open, standing in farmyards talking about the
prices of cattle cake, grain and fertilizers. At the weekends
he played full-back for a Berwickshire rugby team. He was
twenty-nine, a big dark young man with a ruddy complexion
and blue eyes. He went out with the boys several nights a
week. Bella's father, owner of a good-going small builder's
business, kept saying: 'It's high time you stopped playin'
rugger, Rod, and did some tackling in your own back yard.'

Rod always said he'd retire from rugger when he was
thirty. 'And then it'll be up to Bella.'

This year he was going to Jugoslavia for a holiday with
some of his team-mates. 'It'll be my last fling with the boys,
Mr Logan.'

Last year Bella had gone abroad for the first time. She
and Rod went to Majorca, but what between Rod's amor-
ousness, brought on by the strong sunshine and the Spanish
atmosphere, and the food not agreeing with her finicky
stomach, she had not enjoyed herself. This year she was
going to be a devil, though, and give abroad another chance:
she and Peggy Allardyce, her best friend, were going to
Venice for a fortnight in September.

Peggy Allardyce, who ran one of the cash-desks, had taken

over the enquiry desk while Bella was at lunch. 'My, you've got a fine cosy wee corner here, dear,' she said when her friend returned. 'It's real groovy, and I love it. You're a right lucky-bag, Bell.'

Bella made a face, but she said nothing. She started to shrug out of her cardigan while watching Peggy click-clack on high heels towards the exit. But she had scarcely sat down at the desk before she quickly pulled the cardigan back on. It was chillier here than outside. She picked up her bag of knitting. There were few customers in the supermarket at this hour, and it was hardly likely anybody would stop to ask her anything. As she was counting her stitches some-body placed a dead-cold finger on her forehead and pressed it into her skull. The pain and the cold were excruciating. Then the finger moved backwards over her skull and down her spine. As it moved, icy waves swept over the rest of her body. She gasped for breath and huddled her cardigan tighter around her.

The rain was coming down in torrents. She clung to the bars of the cage with hands so frozen she was sure the skin would come off if she let go of the iron. Her palms burned. Her saturated gown clung to her body, encasing her like armour. The cage had been pulled up higher; it hung now about ten feet from the ground. The downpour had driven away most of the crowd who came to gloat, but many women had taken refuge from the deluge in doorways and windows, from whence their gimlet-brimstone eyes probed into her humiliation and their frog-gawped mouths opened to shout insults. Among them were the old witch with the dirty white hair who came every day and the red-headed youth who was always with her. The English sentries still stood around the cage. They were almost as soaked as she was, but every now and then they took turns to escape into an embrasure in the castle walls and sheltered there for a while.

She had been in the cage for seven days and seven nights. She was fed and watered like an animal, but the cage was never mucked out. She thought of what they had done to

William Wallace at Smithfield last year. Fine handsome Sir William who had endured such degradation and agony before death mercifully came. She remembered Sir William, after the battle of Stirling Bridge, coming to Methven Castle to discuss his campaign against the English with her father, the old Earl of Fife. She had been but a child in that year 1297 but she had fallen in love a little with the handsome knight. She closed her eyes. A quarter of his tortured, dismembered body had been displayed here in Berwick last year. She wondered if her own head might not grace a spike on Berwick's walls, unless Edward, the so-called Hammer of the Scots, God rot him, considered it important enough to flaunt on London Bridge.

She clasped her hands around her neck and shuddered.

'The braw leddy's pee-ed hersel'!' the white-haired witch shrilled. 'See ye! The grand leddy's water is juist like yours and mine.'

After a time the rain slackened. It turned into a drizzle. She wanted to shake her shoulders to ease away the dress clinging to her back, but she would not do this before the rabble. She was gazing upwards, intent on ignoring all taunts, when there was a creaking of the chains by which the cage was suspended. It began to come down. Its descent was so uneven that she was forced to grip the bars to steady herself. It was about shoulder-high from the ground when a scullion ran from the castle gate carrying a plate of food. He thrust the plate through the bars and emptied its mess of boiled oatmeal and pieces of half-raw meat on to the floor.

'Eat hearty, my lady!' he jeered before running back to the gate.

A big brosy-faced soldier standing in the embrasure laughed. He fumbled with his crotch and shouted: 'Wouldst like a taste of this meat, lady? Put thy hand through the bars and grasp it.'

She turned her back on him, but this made her face the doorway in which the old witch and the red-headed youth were sheltering. The youth put his hand between his legs and imitated the soldier, shouting lewd remarks.

She had such a convulsion of disgust that her entrails seemed to rush in icy globules up to her throat. A great wave of terror coursed through her. Bella did not know whether she screamed or not. She came back to the present, clutching her throat. Someone was making spine-shuddering scratching noises on the glass of the enquiry desk.

A tall thin gangling youth with greasy carroty hair hanging well below his narrow shoulders was leering at her. 'How ye doin', Miss Logan?' he mouthed. The wisps of his straggly moustache and beard could not hide the blackened stumps between his yellowed teeth. 'Gettin' on all right then?'

'I'm managing quaite well, thankew, Zander,' Bella said, giving him a cold nod.

'Well, ye know where to apply if ye want anythin',' he leered. 'If ye get into any trouble, Miss Logan – er, Bella, d'ye mind? – juist you give me a wee shout and I'll be here at the toot.'

'I don't think I am likely to have any trouble, thankew, Zander,' she said through pursed lips. 'I am quaite capable of looking after myself, if I may say so.'

Zander gave her a mock salute and, sidling and squirming, said: 'Well, duty calls! I'd better get crackin', Bella, or I'll have auld Stott on my top. See ya, Bella!' He gave a high screeching giggle and wavered away.

Though Bella fought against them, trying not to think of them, the nightmares or hallucinations continued. Every day, at different times, sometimes once, sometimes twice, she would be dragged back by a gigantic ice-cold hand into that iron cage with its smell of excrement, and see again those gloating, pitiless faces revelling in her humiliation. And then, wondering if she could endure another minute of the agony, she would be dragged back as suddenly into the present, and with frozen hands and feet and a cold dread at her heart she would tell herself that probably she was sickening for influenza.

Bella told nobody about these experiences for fear of be-

ing laughed at. She felt she should tell her mother, but she
was afraid Mrs Logan would whisk her off to the doctor. As
it was, Mrs Logan said one lunchtime after the uncanny
happenings had been going on for about a week: 'You're
off your food, dear. I'm wondering if your new job agrees
with you. You're looking kind of peakit.'

Bella assured her mother she was all right, and she forced
herself to eat what was put in front of her. Ten days after
the supermarket opened, she did something she had never
done in her life. On her half-day she went to the Public
Library. She was there for three hours, looking at books an
assistant librarian kept bringing to her. 'What does little
Miss Prim want?' asked another assistant, an auburn-haired
girl who had been at school with Bella, though they never
acknowledged each other when they met.

'She wants something about the history of Berwick.'

The auburn-haired girl sniffed. 'Can she read? It's the
first I've ever heard tell of it.'

At last, after looking through a great many volumes,
Bella discovered that Berwick's ancient castle stood once
where the railway station was built. Many atrocities had
taken place in the castle. One was the hanging from its walls
in July 1306 of a cage imprisoning Isabella, the beautiful
young Countess of Buchan. This punishment had been
ordered by King Edward I of England because the Countess,
acting as the representative of her brother, the Earl of Fife,
who was Edward's prisoner at the time, had crowned Robert
the Bruce as King of Scotland at Scone. The Countess had
been kept in this cage for four years, then she had been removed to another prison, and her end was not known.

On her way to meet Peggy Allardyce, Bella tried to imagine what the Countess of Buchan must have felt like after
four years of being battered by the elements and the even
more merciless crowd, but even with what she had experienced in her own supernatural flights, if indeed they were
supernatural, she could not picture what state Isabella of
Buchan must have been in by the time she was taken to another prison. Before she reached the café in the Scotsgate

where Peggy was waiting, Bella had turned her mind to the dress she would wear at the rugger club dance the following Saturday night.

That evening she considered confiding in her mother, but after a lot of deliberation she decided against it. She knew her mother would either laugh and tell her she was daft, or she would insist on taking her to the doctor. One thing Bella was aware of, however. Every time she experienced the terrors of the cage she had noticed that either old Mrs Cessford or her gangling grandson was in contact with her before or after the happening.

Next morning, fighting against the chill creeping up her legs, she saw with a sense of fatality Mrs Cessford approaching the enquiry desk.

'Can I have a word with ye, hen?' The witch stretched her gap-toothed mouth into an ingratiating smirk.

Bella stopped knitting and said: 'I suppose so. It's what I'm here for, isn't it?'

'Ye'll have heard about my misfortune, hen?' Mrs Cessford said. 'I swear to you, it wasnie my fault. It was a mistake. I had the money in ma purse. It was juist absent-mindedness that made me put the stockings in ma bag instead o' into the wire-basket wi' the other things I was buyin'.'

'I'm sorry,' Bella said. 'I don't know what you're talking about.'

'But ye've seen the paper surely, hen? It was front page news in the *Berwick Advertiser*: "Elderly Widow Accused of Shoplifting in Woolworths." Ye must have seen it.'

'I never read the papers,' Bella said.

'Well, I tell ye it was a mistake. As sure as I put up ma hand to the livin' God. I would never dream o' doin' sic a low-down dirty trick. I tellt the magistrates that, but they wouldnie listen. They juist said: "Fined ten pounds. Next case." Oh, it was sic an affront! I'll never be able to hold up ma head in our neighbourhood again. So that's why I've come to you. I was wonderin', hen, if yer faither – him that's so big with the Toon Cooncil – could maybe help a puir

auld widow-body. I ken I'm Labour and he's a Scottish
Nationalist, but surely he wouldnie let politics stand between him and helpin' a puir body to get a cooncil hoose.'

'But my father has nothing to do with the Town
Council,' Bella said. 'He only does contract work for them
occasionally.'

'Oh, but he's got their ears all right. And a word in the
right direction is all I want. You speir him for me, will ye,
hen?' Mrs Cessford whined.

'I'm sorry,' Bella said, 'I know my father couldn't do it,
and I'm not going to ask him.'

'Oh, but ye're a prideful wee madam!' Mrs Cessford's
small black eyes blazed. 'Ye wouldnie lift a finger to help a
puir auld widdy. It's a pity I asked ye. I should ha'e kent
better after the way ye've treated my grandson, him that
thinks the world o' ye. I've tellt him often enough that ye're
a stinkin' wee hoor and that he should look elsewhere for a
guid decent lassie.'

'Your grandson is of no interest to me whatever. Now,
will you please go or I'll call the manager?'

'You'll regret this, my braw leddy. You'll live to rue the
day ye crossed Mercy Cessford. I've seen ye canoodlin' in
the back o' his car wi' yon big fitba' player. Ye may think
ye're lucky to be on the pill, but it'll no' aye work. It's nae
mair to be trusted than the french letters we had when I
was young. I juist hope ye get caught, ye wee bitch.'

Bella rose and stepped out of the desk. Mrs Cessford
skirled with spleen and flounced away, shouting: 'Ye'll
regret it! Just mark my words. Ye'll regret it!'

Mouth primmed with disapproval, Bella was settling herself in her chair again when she felt the icy blast sweeping
up from the floor. She stood and held on to the sides of the
desk, fighting against it ...

That night the nightmares followed her home. She went to
bed about midnight, after watching television with her
parents, and fell asleep almost at once.

When she opened her eyes it was pitch-dark. A fiendish

gale from the North Sea was howling around her. The cage was swinging so violently that she had to cling to the bars to steady herself. Sleet and snow enveloped her. Her tattered filthy clothes were clamped to her soaking body. Her wet hair was plastered over her face. She gave great sobbing breaths and pressed against the bars. High above her were wild screams. A flock of seagulls was circling the cage, drawn to it by the stench of excrement and the remains of rotten food.

Then, above the screaming of the seagulls, she heard other unearthly wails. Three figures in snow-encrusted cloaks that caused them to stand out in ghostly manner in the darkness were hovering around the cage. The sentries had taken shelter in the embrasures of the castle walls, knowing nobody would try to rescue her on such a wild night.

'Are ye there, Leddy Bella? Are ye there? Ye're no' sleepin', are ye?'

Mercy Cessford, the witch, pressed her ghastly wizened face against the bars. Her features had a luminous gleam: the long nose and the high cheekbones stood out, shining grotesquely, and a wide black gap showed instead of her nearly toothless mouth.

'We ha'e brocht ye a visitor, hinny,' she cackled. 'A braw visitor for a braw leddy that's no sae braw now as she aince was.'

Isabella shuddered and closed her eyes, trying to blot out the three awesome faces. On one side of the witch was her grandson, the red-haired warlock. On Mistress Cessford's other side was another warlock, a tall man wearing a tall black hat. Amber eyes with a reddish glow burned into her under the frown of his thick black brows.

' 'Tis the Master himself come to visit ye, prood leddy,' the witch said. 'He has come with an offer of freedom.'

'Silence, Mercy,' the warlock cried. 'Let me deal direct with the lady. I do not require your offices of mediation.'

'Isabella of Buchan,' he said. 'I can set you free. Only I, Lucifer, can set you free. But in return I wish your allegiance. Will ye swear to give me that in return for my unlocking

this door and taking you speedily from hence? Whither
wouldst like to go, madam? To your castle at Methven
mayhap, to wallow again in silks and fine raiment, to eat
once more fine cooked meats and dainty sweetmeats?'

Isabella unclasped her hands from the bars and put them
over her ears, trying to deaden the sibilant voice. A violent
gust of wind shook the cage and sent her tumbling to the
floor. She lay there with her arms over her head.

'All I need, lady, is your word,' the devil whispered. 'Your
promise to be my handmaiden sometimes when I need thy
help. I will not be a hard taskmaster. Mayhap I might never
seek thy services. All I require is your oath of allegiance.'

'No, no!' Isabella cried, but her words were whisked away
by the wind.

The Master laughed and whispered: ' 'Tis a small price
to pay for thy freedom, lady.'

'Will ye no' join our coven, Leddy Bella?' cackled the
crone.

'Hold your tongue, Mercy,' the devil ordered. Then
wheedlingly he whispered: 'A silken dress again, a hot per-
fumed bath, meat served on a silver platter . . . What dost
say, Lady Buchan?'

'Go away! Go away!' she screamed. 'Leave me in peace,
you foul fiends!'

The devil laughed, then he and his minions began to fly
around the cage, flapping their arms and making their
cloaks fly out so that they looked like gigantic bats. Bella
screamed and screamed . . .

She awoke in her mother's arms. 'There, there, my wee pet,'
Mrs Logan soothed. 'It was just a bad dream.'

'Mammy, Mammy,' Bella sobbed. 'I can't take it any
longer.'

And it all poured out. Mrs Logan slept with her for the
rest of the night. She would not allow her to go to work.
And she accompanied her to the doctor at half-past ten,
saying: 'Your granny is of the opinion that it must be your

nerves. Maybe the doctor'll prescribe Sanatogen or Win-carnis or something like that.'

Dr Nesbitt gave Bella a thorough examination. At her mother's prompting she told him about having nightmares but did not mention their nature. She admitted that her legs and arms and shoulders ached and that she had unnatural spells of icy coldness. 'There's nothing wrong with your heart and lungs,' Dr Nesbitt said. 'You're as healthy a young woman as I've ever come across. A lassie like you should take more exercise. All that's wrong with you is that your muscles are getting cramped with aye sitting in that confined space. Go for long walks on the golf course or along the banks of the Tweed. Go down to the sands and get the sea breezes into your lungs.'

He gave her a prescription for a tonic and told her to take a week off work.

In that week she had no hallucinations during the days, but every night she had visitations from the demon and his witches. She managed not to waken up screaming, and she contrived to hide it from her mother. Mrs Logan noticed, though, that Bella remained pale and nervous, so she had a word with her husband, who, in turn, had a word with Rod Wishart. 'I suggest,' Mr Logan said, 'that you ask your firm for the new territory they keep promising you, then I think you and our Bella had better put up the banns. The quicker she's away from the climate of Berwick, the happier her mother and me'll be – even if we are going to miss her.'

As soon as Bella returned to the enquiry desk the happenings started again in daylight. She learned, however, to control them a little, making them fainter and farther off, by rising and opening the door of the desk, and she would cling to this while the emanations from the Middle Ages lasted.

One day she was not quick enough. Her mind was so occupied in counting the stitches of a yellow pullover she had started to knit for Rod that the icy waves of terror had swept up from her ankles to her waist before she started to rise. She was forced to sink back into her seat. She clutched

her throat and succumbed to the full blast of the chilling,
cruel medieval dread. . . .

The cage swung high above the crowd, but for once the
harpies in the crowd were not looking and jeering at her.
Most of them had their backs turned. They were watching
two great piles of brushwood and logs. In the centre of each
pile was a stake. Sagging in her own filth and wretchedness,
beaten by the weather, her clothes hanging in sodden tatters,
her hair matted and her skin corroded by wind, rain and
dirt, Isabella of Buchan saw the old witch, Mercy Cessford,
and her grandson being dragged through the crowd by hefty
English soldiers. They were tied to the stakes. The old witch
screamed imprecations all the time, but the young warlock
was able only to gibber. For once, the crowd was silent.
There were no jeers and taunts like those usually directed
against the Countess. Some women were weeping. Many
must have been thinking: 'There but for the grace of
God . . .'

A herald proclaimed: 'Hear ye! Hear ye, citizens of
Berwick! Whereas the perfidious witch, Mistress Mercy
Cessford and her demoralized grandson, the warlock Zander
Cessford, have perpetrated divers cantrips and incantations
against the person of His Majesty, King Edward the First of
England, Scotland and Wales and the territories beyond,
His Majesty has decreed that the said witch and the said
warlock shall meet their deaths by burning. And may God
have mercy on their souls!'

A sigh of despair rose from the crowd, and there were
some half muffled shouts of protest when fiery torches were
thrust into the pyres. Isabella leant her forehead against a
cold iron bar and sighed with the crowd. As the first thin
smoke came through the brushwood, the old witch looked
up at the cage and keened: ' 'Tis thy fault, prood Bella, for
not doin' what the Master askit. And 'tis thy fault for
crownin' the Bruce and bringin' the wrath of King Edward
upon us. Ye will regret thy work for centuries to come. My
dyin' curse on ye, prood leddy.'

And then the old woman started to scream again. Isabella

closed her eyes. The woman's screams turned into throat-strangling retches. The warlock shrieked every few seconds. But gradually the screams became fainter and, finally, ceased. When Isabella opened her eyes she could see nothing but the flames and, above them, great clouds of dark grey and black smoke. Swirls of wind blew the smoke into the cage. Her eyes were stung, her nostrils filled, her throat seared by the salt of strong iron tongues being thrust into them. Isabella started to cough. She clutched her throat and struggled against the billows of smoke....

Bella coughed and coughed, her throat scalded by the sour-sweet clutch of wood smoke, until she slumped in a heap on the enquiry desk. She recovered consciousness lying on the floor with her head on a folded rug that had been taken from a pram. The infant in the pram was yelling with temper. Its mother, her back turned to it, was leaning against the pram shoogling it, her mouth half-open, looking at Bella and Mr Stott and the spectators who had gathered.

'I want my mother,' Bella gasped. 'I want—'

'Now now, Miss Logan, take it easy,' Mr Stott murmured in agitation, on his hunkers beside her. 'We'll get you sent home presently. You seem to have had a wee turn, but you'll soon be all right. I would take you home myself, but I can't leave the market. I'll get somebody else to take you in their car in a minute.'

That evening Peggy Allardyce came to see Bella in bed. 'Isn't it awful,' she said when she had finished commiserating with her friend, 'there's been a terrible fire in Percy's Vennel and two folk were burned to death. Auld Mrs Cessford and her grandson Zander. You know him, Bell, don't you? Yon nice laddie with the ginger hair that does odd jobs like filling the shelves and sweeping the floor. Poor soul! What a dreadful death!'

'Yes, isn't it?' Bella said, handing Peggy a knitting pattern. 'D'you like this, Peg? I think it would be smashing in powder-blue and white.'

'What's this I hear?' Rod said when Mrs Logan showed

him into Bella's bedroom later on. 'I hear you fainted in the street and the Fire Brigade had to be called out. And fancy being brought home in a police car!'

'Funny, aren't you?' Bella said.

'Never mind, dear,' he said. 'Your fainting days are over. I heard this morning that the firm are putting me in charge of their Perth territory, so we'd better get spliced. Okay by you?'

Bella gave a little nod and said: 'I suppose so.'

She made no objection next morning when her mother would not allow her to return to work. She wrote a short note to Mr Stott, giving in her notice.

In the next few weeks, getting ready for her wedding, she did not have time to think about her other-worldly experiences, except one evening when she was approaching the supermarket to meet Peggy and she had a faint emanation of once again standing in the cage with the wind and the witch and the warlocks whirling around her.

But she was aware of much more than a faint emanation on the evening that Rod announced that his firm had got them a house near Perth. 'It's at Methven, about ten miles from Perth,' he said. 'A very nice house I hear, with four bedrooms, a lounge, a kitchen, bathroom and two lavatories, and all the usual. It's built where the ruins of Methven Castle used to stand.'

Bella heard no more. The ice-cold terror swept over her again, and she found herself on the back of a prancing horse while the clash of battle raged all around her. She was watching a tall man in armour on a black horse. He had a circlet of gold on his helmet, and the June sunlight sent sparks from it as he galloped full tilt against some English knights. Beyond the battlefield she could see her father's castle of Methven, and she was still gazing towards its towers when the English soldiers surrounded her and took her prisoner.

THE HORSESHOE INN

The girl behind the reception counter of the Horseshoe Inn, which stood halfway up Quarry Hill just outside Dalwhinnie, recognized Jackie Caskie as soon as he came through the side door from the motor hotel's car-park. She wasn't a sports fan but his face had been on the front page of the Glasgow papers that morning, yet another of the many sensations and scandals involving the controversial Glasgow Star. Pushing in the drawer she had been emptying she said, blushingly:

'I'm awfully sorry, sir, we're closed down.'

Jackie Caskie's widely-set blue eyes did not blink, nor was there any suggestion of a smile about his prematurely hardened face.

'It doesnae say the place is shut,' he said, nodding in the direction of the forecourt.

'We put a notice out . . .'

'Got a manager?' he snapped. His upper lip did not move when he spoke, his lower lip only slightly. It was the hardness of his mouth which betrayed his young man's ruddy cheeks.

The girl, Janet, went through to the small, windowless office where McIver the manager was sorting out unpaid bills and invoices for the accountants who were winding up the company. Closing the door she said, 'Eh, Mr McIver, Jackie Caskie's at the desk, I think he wants to book in.'

McIver stared at her stupidly, mouth open. He was a middle-aged man with a narrow, fleshy face, given to little grins, which most people assumed to denote failure, an impression reinforced by his rounded shoulders and slightly furtive manner. She nodded dramatically. 'I told him we weren't open any more . . .'

'Jackie Caskie?' he said, frowning. 'Are you sure?'

'Oh yes, couldn't mistake him.' She leaned forward, lowering her voice. 'He doesn't seem very nice.'

'Jackie Caskie? No, he isn't very *nice*, if it is him. Well well well.' He shook his head.

'Shall I tell him again we're closed?'

McIver shrugged. Then he smiled. He stood up and lifted his shabby jacket off the back of the swivel chair, raising one eyebrow in debonair manner as he brushed cigarette ash off the dark serge and tightened the knot of his grubby Terylene tie. 'A famous star would expect to have the personal attention of the manager. Is he drunk?'

'I don't think so. It is only half-past eleven in the morning.'

'My dear girl, a big star like Jackie Caskie isn't fettered by mere licensing hours.'

'Do you know him, do you?'

'We met once, some years ago,' McIver said drily. 'I don't suppose *he'll* remember though.'

He stepped out into the reception area, both eyebrows raised.

'This is a rare honour indeed for us here in the back of beyond,' he said, putting on his 'grand' or professional voice. Caskie appraised him with a glance, obviously marking him down as an unimportant flunkey, a type of man he had feared as a boy then learned to use as a celebrity but had always despised.

'I'm on my way to Manchester,' he said in his harsh Glasgow voice, 'I need to stay here the day, I never got tae bed all last night so I'm dropping asleep at the wheel.'

McIver ran his tongue round his front teeth. 'Now that's a trifle awkward – we've just gone out of business. We're too near Glasgow for the motorway trade and with this recession . . .'

Caskie stared at him blankly, confident that his fame would bend the rules, as always. And he was right, although not for the reason he assumed. Suddenly smiling with the bravado of a normally timid man who has at last dared to accept a risky challenge, McIver said, 'But we do have fourteen bedrooms doing nothing. Is your car outside?'

'Round the back – I put it out of sight in case there's any reporters tailing me.'

Travelling the world on the glamour circuit hadn't even begun to dent Caskie's crude vowels and the glottal stops and total lack of the normal inflexions. A roughneck from the coarse element of Glasgow. He was wearing a black roll-neck sweater under a tweed jacket of modern cut in a bright black and white check, a gold watch on his wrist, two or three rings on his fingers. He was about five feet eight, aggressively fit in appearance, chest sticking out under the black sweater, bulging calf muscles pushing against his grey flannel trousers, legs slightly bowed. Neither the physical fitness nor the expensive clothes nor the professionally-styled black curls could hide his origins, however.

'We met before, about ten years ago,' McIver said, 'you probably don't remember, I was a trainee under-manager at the New Scotia Hotel . . .'

'Thought I knew your face,' Caskie said dismissively. He'd dealt with flunkeys and lackeys all over the world and rarely bothered to listen to the ingratiating words. If you had a famous face they would crawl all over your boots, although he knew damn well they sneered at him behind his back for being a common Glasgow moron, somebody they would have shown the door if he had not been a star. There was a time when he'd enjoyed making them jump to it, especially the toffee-nosed ones with the high-falutin' accents, but he didn't have to throw his weight about these days. They jumped anyway, as soon as they saw his face.

'Is there anything you want to get from your car?' McIver asked. It did not surprise him when Caskie dropped his car-keys on the counter and said he had a leather hold-all on the back seat. Big stars never fetched their own luggage. McIver took the keys and went outside. It had been a sunny morning but dark clouds were spreading from Ayrshire and the Atlantic. The big bleak hill behind the motor hotel was already looking dark and hostile. Half a mile away on the other side of the valley he could see the tops of cars and vans on the motorway, the perpetual race to nowhere as he called it, being slightly more philosophical than most people gave him credit for – deep even.

Naturally the car was a big red Jaguar, the slum boy showing off his fame and money. He sniffed as he leaned across the seat. Yes, a definite trace of booze. Well well well – after all these years, to catch up with Jackie Caskie again.

Before he went inside he crossed the forecourt to the entrance off the old main road and found the Closed sign lying on its face. He put it back in position.

In the foyer he found Caskie giving Janet the benefit of his personality. As seduction patter it was hardly subtle – 'no' much to do at nights in a dump like this, eh?' – but sporting heroes seldom needed to over-exert themselves in these matters. He noted, with the dispassionate envy of a man who has accepted middle age, that prim little Janet was not mentioning any unbreakable date she might have with her fiancé, a drip of a student-teacher called Norrie Barr, whose father was a licensed grocer in Dalwhinnie. However, he had heard her arranging for Norrie to pick her up at two o'clock and said, silently, to Caskie, You're wasting your charm there, friend, if charm is the word.

'I'll show you the rooms,' he said. 'By the way, welcome to the Horseshoe Inn.'

'Funny name for a motel,' Caskie said, winking at Janet.

'There was a pub on this site,' McIver said, 'it had a cobbled yard with a horseshoe set in the middle – it was to mark the site of the gallows where they hung the Dalwhinnie martyrs.'

'Unlucky for some. Who'd they find tae hang in a wee joint like this?'

'Covenanters. About three hundred years ago. Seemingly all these small towns had their own hangman in those days. Probably the only entertainment they got – plus burning witches.'

'Thank God for the television then,' Caskie joked, for Janet's benefit. As they went into the corridor he winked at her and said, 'Don't run away, I'll buy you a drink.'

As McIver showed him empty rooms he explained that the directors had only decided to close the place on the previous Friday and still had hopes of selling it as a going concern. Caskie wasn't interested. He said he would take Room 27, immediately asking where the bar was. The liquor store was locked and anything taken now would mean writing out a new stock-list for the valuers but McIver said he would open the Sheiling Bar, a favour which Caskie did not acknowledge with even a token remark of gratitude. When Caskie asked Janet to join them in the deserted bar she looked at McIver, who said, 'Not every day you lose a job *and* meet one of Scotland's heroes, you might as well mark the occasion with a drop of vintage Babycham.'

Before McIver had the bottles out of the stock-room – American whisky for Caskie, malt whisky for himself and Tio Pepe for Janet – rain was battering on the big picture windows. In the presence of the girl Caskie became quite humorous, telling them bits of scandal about various celebrities who were great friends of his, concentrating his attention on Janet, whose reaction of shock and disbelief mingled with obvious enthusiasm for such intimacy with the celebrity made her the ideal audience. After ten minutes McIver told himself he knew what Caskie's trouble was – only a man heading in the direction of alcoholism threw them over *that* quickly.

'Just leave the bottle for God's sake,' Caskie said when McIver re-filled his glass for the third time, 'I'll see you all right, chief.'

'Be my guest,' McIver said airily, himself still cautiously sipping his first ball of Glenlivet. Two Tio Pepes and Janet was showing signs of giggles. When Norrie Barr turned up at two o'clock Caskie insisted that he joined them in a drink, ignoring the look on Norrie's face. McIver was amused. Prim little Janet was clearly wishing she had not arranged to drive to Dumfries with Norrie, while Norrie, give him credit, revealed a tougher edge than McIver had suspected in the mother's boy. He took a small whisky and lemonade without saying much, waiting until the laughter had died down after another of Caskie's anecdotes.

'The papers say you've walked out on your wife and your contract – is that right?'

Consciously or not, Caskie was by then doing a fair imitation of James Cagney. With a wave of his hand and a dismissive snort he said, 'The papers know nothing, kid. I've been through Hell in the last two years, absolute Hell.' He put his hand on Janet's knee and peered sadly into her face. 'My wife understands me all too well, darling, can you give me any good advice?'

'You're a caution, so you are,' Janet said with mock-disapproval. Caskie's hand stayed on her knee. McIver sipped his malt.

'The papers also say you're leaving Scotland for good,' Norrie said coldly.

'Why not?' Caskie snapped. 'What has Scotland done for me? You think I owe any loyalty to all them bums? Oh aye, they say they love you when you're at the top but just wait till you start slipping – then the knives are out. I owe nobody nothing.'

'You've done well for yourself though, you must admit,' McIver said sympathetically.

'Oh sure. Got a forty-thousand-pound house in Midlothian, two cars, thirty suits, a good few grand in the bank, a million friends, invitations to go everywhere if I wanted to accept – oh sure. But what's in it for me, eh? I mean me . . .' he tapped his chest, glaring aggressively at Norrie and then McIver . . . 'I know the truth. Deep down they hate me because I'm successful. They hate successful people in this rotten country, they're just dying for the moment when you start sliding and they can tear you apart. The hell with 'em. I'm going down tae England, too bloody true I am, they'll maybe appreciate me a bit more down there.'

'What about your contract?' Norrie asked.

His persistence was beginning to annoy Caskie. He put his index finger against Norrie's chest, smiling bleakly in what McIver knew was part of the ritual preparation for outright aggression.

'Sonny,' he said quietly, 'contracts are only bits of paper. Money counts, that's all. My manager says I'll never appear in public again because he's got my signature on a bit of paper? Managers? Bloody parasites. He'll cave in soon as he gets the message.'

To McIver's surprise Janet revealed a streak of common-sense at that dangerous moment. Getting off her stool she said, 'It's been very nice meeting you, Jackie, but Norrie and I have to go now . . .'

'Ach, have another drink,' Caskie said, snapping finger and thumb in McIver's direction.

'No, we're late as it is, we're looking at a house in case Norrie takes a job in Dumfries,' Janet said.

'No' just one more for the road?' Caskie said, pleadingly.

But no, prim little Janet had made up her mind. McIver locked the side door behind them and went back into the Sheiling Bar. Caskie was staring morosely at the rain-swept windows. 'She looks like a typical dull wee housewife already,' he snarled. 'See him? Read a few books and they think they're above us common rubbish. Make ye sick. Having a drink, are you?'

'Why not?' said McIver. 'Nobody's waiting for me to go anywhere.'

Caskie did not respond. Sipping what was only his second malt McIver studied the younger man, recognizing the familiar egomania that went with fame. Caskie was as demanding as an infant or a beautiful woman in his need for attention. Last year wasn't a time when miners died in pit explosions or the Nationalists won an election or an influential bureaucrat went to prison but a date to hang on some triumph of Caskie's. The country wasn't going to the dogs through unemployment, inflation or high taxation – things were bad because *Caskie* was paying too much in tax, because *Caskie*'s various sideline businesses were faltering, because *Caskie*'s car had been savagely vandalized by teenage hooligans. If he had any attitude to the rest of the world it was of cynicism or contempt. The public he regarded as dangerous morons.

'We'll support ye ever more, you'll hear them singing their hearts out, tears in their eyes. Oh aye, they'll die for Scotland, so they will. And I'm supposed to be loyal to *that*? Lot of half-drunk eejits. Cannae support themselves let alone Scotland.'

He was drinking more slowly now, staring moodily out of the big window at the storm, apparently conversing with McIver simply from lack of better company.

Struck by some inspiration he suddenly asked where the phone was.

'It's been cut off, I'm afraid,' McIver said.

'Nae phone? Funny way to run a hotel.'

'We're not actually running a hotel, though,' McIver said, without any note of apology, 'we've closed down, remember?'

'Oh aye, so you have.'

They sat for another half-hour in the gloom of the big empty bar, their voices droning through the tartan-bedecked walls and across the shiny table-tops. At last McIver could hold it in no longer.

'You once did me a bit of a dirty turn,' he said pleasantly, 'I served you once with a round of drinks after hours in the New Scotia Hotel. I was just learning the trade then and I was a bit nervous serving you and your famous friends – I spilled a big whisky on your trousers.'

'That right?' Caskie said, uninterested.

'You sent for the manager and said you wanted me sacked.'

'Yeah? Did he do it?'

'No, but he docked my wages for the price of a round *and* the cleaning of your trousers.'

Caskie snorted with faint amusement. 'Aye, I do get a bit fed up with bad service. Got any grub in this deserted graveyard?

McIver brought out a few packets of bacon and onion flavoured crisps. Caskie ate them as previously he had downed drinks, throwing them down by the handful. On one of his visits to the lavatory McIver ate his sandwiches.

To his reflection in the mirror he said, 'Who said life was supposed to be fair?'

The afternoon grew darker. He switched on the soft lights of the bar gantry. Food in his stomach made him warmer and when he looked at Caskie he felt sorry – and puzzled. Two million Scotsmen would probably say Caskie had the dream life, talent, fame, money, success – and yet he seemed well set on the traditional road to self-destruction. In a way he began to feel fatherly. The man was an illiterate lout but very likely he had never been given any encouragement to be anything else. Maybe the right word spoken now ...

'Tell me if I'm poking my nose in, Jackie,' he said, 'but this running away – and all the other things you've been involved in – don't you think you've been very lucky? I mean, you couldn't really ask for more, could you? Fame, success, money ...'

'And women?' Caskie sneered. 'You're right, I've had hundreds. Throw themselves at you if you're famous – no' just wee hairies either but doctors' wives, millionaires' daughters – we're sex symbols so we are.' He snorted. Then he looked at McIver and said, with the unabashed eyes of a cheeky boy, 'But you wouldn't be interested in women, would you?'

'What does that mean?'

'It doesnae bother me, chief, wherever you get your kicks, that's what I say.'

McIver almost choked. The sheer injustice of it! To be humiliated twice in one lifetime by this same big-headed, uneducated, self-glorifying moron! A man who had the morals of an abattoir rat! But for the fact that he'd now had five whiskies he would have walked out on Caskie, got in his own car and driven off.

Instead he lifted Caskie's bottle and said, 'This one's about finished – want another bottle out the store?'

'Might as well,' Caskie said, his voice only slightly slurred, 'a couple more and I'll turn in.'

In the store-room McIver closed his eyes and clenched his fists ...

It was about half-past eight, the wind battering at the big windows, the storm so dark they could not see the lights of Dalwhinnie across the valley, when McIver said casually, 'Funny business that hanging I told you about, the Dalwhinnie martyrs. It was in 1666, six men from Dalwhinnie were charged with being Covenanters and sentenced to be hung for rebellion . . .'

'Ach, history gives me the scunner, I hated it at school . . .'

'This is interesting though – the Dalwhinnie hangman refused to do the job, he was frightened of what the town people would do to him afterwards – or maybe he agreed with them. So you know what the Provost did? They tried to get the hangmen from two or three other towns to come and put the noose round them but they all refused. So the Provost said to the six, "If one of you will hang the other five he can go free." At first they all refused.'

'That a fact?' said Caskie, blurred eyes blinking slowly. 'They must've been mugs.'

'But after a wee while in the gloomy dungeon one of them asked to see the Provost and said he would do it. How about that? He would hang his best friends – a man who'd risked his life to give Scotland the right to worship God its own way? A psalm-singing, Bible-reading Christian? Would *you* have done it – to save your own neck?'

Caskie swayed on his stool. 'Sure I would! Look out for number one, that's the rule.'

McIver nodded slowly. 'I've often wondered myself what I would have done. Anyway, this Judas gets cold feet half way through the night – they're hanging them first thing in the morning – and says he's chickening out. So the Provost sends for bottles of brandy and gets him drunk and keeps him well stocked up till dawn. And he did it then!'

'I wonder if he said sorry,' Caskie rasped, falling about at his own wit.

'Aye, I've wondered what he said to them often enough. You know the funny thing, however – his name was Caskie. Well, McCaskie actually. James McCaskie – same name as yourself.'

'Christ! You joking?'

'No. There's a local poem about him – Judas McCaskie
they call him. They say he used to haunt the old pub that
was here, his soul trying to get somebody to forgive him.
I've always been told the locals took him out on the moors
and stoned him to death and dug a hole for him.' McIver
laughed. The sound echoed among the crossed swords and
embossed shields on the walls between the tartan plaques.
Caskie's face stared white and shocked in the diffused light
from the gantry. 'Maybe he was an ancestor of yours,'
McIver said cheerfully.

'Of course he wasnae,' Caskie protested. 'Christ, what did
ye tell me that for?'

'Thought you'd be interested. I'll be back in a jiffy.'

Caskie shook himself and unsteadily poured himself another rye whisky. 'Ach, lot of old fairy tales,' he said, out
loud. He shivered. 'This place was a mistake. I'll ask that
creepy bastard if he'll drive me into the town, book in at a
normal pub, hullo folks, Jackie Caskie's here! Aye, that's
the clever thing to do here, Jackie boy.'

He got off his stool and lurched, steadying himself against
the bar. He had to screw up his eyes to see the time on his
watch. Five to nine. Plenty of time for a few drinks in some
place with bright lights and a bit of company. He didn't
fancy spending the night alone in this funeral parlour with
that creep. 'Hey, Jimmy?' he said loudly, vaguely realizing
he didn't know the manager's name. He walked carefully
to the end of the bar and called into the corridor. 'Are you
there, chief?' There was no reply. He staggered through the
corridor to the washroom but the manager wasn't in there.
He ran the cold tap and hung his head over the basin until
the impact of the water cleared his brain. What he needed
was a big steak and a pint of ale, get the taste of this place
out of his mouth. Wiping himself carefully he straightened
up and went back to the bar, walking briskly with only a
slight bump against the wall to show that he'd been drinking
all day. The bar was deserted.

'Where are you for God's sake?' he yelled.

A loud but muffled voice spoke at him from every direction at once. 'Judas Caskie, your time has come,' it said.

He spotted the tannoy speakers and lost his temper. 'Stop playing silly kids' games,' he shouted, pouring himself another drink.

'You hung my brother, Judas Caskie,' said the deep, metallic voice.

'I'll hang you into the bargain if you don't show your face,' Caskie shouted. The voice laughed. Caskie took a drink and then headed back into the corridor, trying to remember where the foyer was. He was going to stick one on that geek, dirty old pervert.

He hit his face against a door-jamb so heavily he reeled about in the dark, groaning with pain. That did it! He held his hands out in front as he felt for the wall, moving along sideways until he could feel the door handle. He opened the door into more darkness. He felt for a light switch. The light revealed that he was in one of the empty bedrooms. He went back into the corridor. Suddenly the voice spoke again.

'We threw big stones at you until your brains were spattered on the heather,' it said, laughing deeply. 'God help you, Judas Caskie. Death to traitors!'

'Death to you, bloody nutcase!' Then Caskie remembered where the reception desk was, through the other door out of the bar. That was where the mike for the public address system would be. When he caught up with the manager he was going to hammer him silly.

'My name is Robert McIver,' said the booming voice, 'you hung me and my brother George, Judas Caskie. You hung five of us, Judas Caskie, may your soul rot in hell.'

Lurching across the deserted bar Caskie muttered, 'Aye and I'm going tae hang you again, pal.'

The lights on the gantry went out as he was going round a table to reach the glass doors. In his panic he careered into a tubular steel chair, crashing to the floor on top of it.

His face hit the hard, slippy carpet. He felt no pain but for a few moments he was too dazed to remember where he was. He thought he heard the crowds shouting at him to get

up. But it was dark. The thought crossed his mind that he
was dying, or had actually died. But I'm only a young man,
he said pleadingly to the unseen eyes.

Cautiously moving his hand he felt cold, smooth metal.
He pushed his legs out and felt the chair moving away from
him. Suddenly he remembered. Rising quickly he banged
his head on the hard edge of the table. He cursed viciously
but kept his balance. The fall had disorientated him but
there was a faint shine from the big windows to provide a
clue to his position. Moving slowly, one step at a time, hands
feeling forward into the darkness, he made his way to the
wall and then to the glass doors.

He pushed them open and felt his way into the corridor,
immediately kicking over something heavy, a fire extin-
guisher or a sand-filled ash-tray. He stood motionless, listening for the manager's movements, hearing only the roaring
whistle of the wind. He moved on carefully, trying to remember the lay-out. He felt bruised and sick and near to
tears with frustration, only the savage thoughts of what he
would do to the manager preventing him from slumping to
the floor in despair.

His hands came to a corner. He knew where he was now.
He leaned out – yes, the reception counter! Was there a
flap? His fingers felt along the underside. He felt the crack
and pushed up.

He crossed the narrow space behind the counter, trying
to make no sound as his hands felt out for the wall. His
fingertips touched wood. He stopped for a moment as a
wave of nausea passed through his head. His legs were
aching.

From behind him the voice said, 'Prepare to meet thy
doom, Judas Caskie.'

His fingers closed round the doorknob. Turning it quickly
he threw the door open and twisted his hand sideways to
switch on the light.

Nothing happened. He flicked the switch up and down
but the manager's office remained in darkness.

Suddenly he was frightened. In his panic he grabbed out

at the darkness, hands bumping into the hatstand, which he immediately hurled across the room.

It crashed against the desk. 'I'll kill you,' he growled. Silence. The roof made creaking noises under the fierce wind. He stood there, trembling.

'Come on,' he said tentatively, 'you've had your joke, put on the lights and we'll forget it, eh?'

Silence.

Then the boom of the metallic voice again. Only this time it was singing 'The Lord's My Shepherd'. Caskie screamed at it to stop. In the middle of a line the voice broke into manic laughter. Caskie started to run towards it but hit the door-jamb with an impact that jarred his whole body.

'Oh God,' he moaned, his jaw shaking uncontrollably. Slowly he collapsed to his knees. The voice spoke from all round him.

'You are doomed, Judas Caskie, your soul will rot in . . .'

There was a low moaning sound and then nothing. Caskie began to cry. 'I never hung anybody,' he gasped through his sobs. 'Oh God what did I do to deserve this?'

After a while his chest stopped heaving. He stood up and wearily began to feel his way to the wall and through the door.

Seeing the faint shine of the glass doors at the other end of the foyer he moved slowly towards the front entrance, telling himself that all he had to do was get in his car and drive away but too dazed and weary to feel excited at this simple solution.

The gale hit him as soon as the door opened. Rain drove against his face. He stumbled on the low steps but regained his balance, holding his head down to shield his eyes. He was walking on gravel. After a moment or two his eyes adjusted enough for him to see the vague outline of the motor hotel, a low building with white walls. The force of the wind made it difficult to breathe. He sensed that he'd reached the corner and turned his back on the wind to head to the concrete yard where he'd parked the car. The gale pushed at his back as if trying to test the strength of his legs.

It seemed like a miracle when he found himself bumping into his car. His hands felt over the wet paintwork, down the glass of the window – and then he was inside, out of the rain, safe from the madman. He sat with his head slumped on his chest, breathing in shallow, staccato gasps.

'Nobody'll ever believe this,' he said out loud.

He switched on the reading light and looked for the ignition keys. They weren't in the dashboard. He felt in his pockets, all the aches and bruises making each movement a wincing ordeal.

The keys weren't in his pocket!

Hell! He'd given them to that bloody mad manager to fetch his bag!

'Oh no,' he moaned, face contorting in tears, 'dear God, I can't take any more.'

Then he remembered the torch in the glove-box. Suddenly he felt an upsurge of energy. It was a big torch in a heavy rubber casing. 'I've got you now, pal,' he muttered viciously, opening the door and stepping up into the wind and rain again.

As soon as the torch showed him the walls of the motor hotel he started to run. He lost his footing on the gravel and fell forward. Raindrops slanted through the beam of the torch. Picking it up he told himself he must still be a bit drunk.

He was limping when he came back into the foyer, the torch in his left hand, his right hand steadying him against the walls. He began to search the hotel, room by room, always listening for the voice to start up again, the circle of light sliding over walls and tables.

In the manager's office he tried the telephone but it was dead. Coming back out of the office the torchlight passed over a man's shoe. He stopped. The circle moved up a trouser leg.

Then it came to the face of the manager.

The eyes were open but they didn't blink or move. Caskie let out a long, low moaning noise.

The manager was crouched under the reception counter,

a space just big enough to take a man with his knees up to his chest. His right arm had fallen sideways on to the carpet. The speaker for the public address system was still in his hand.

'Dear Jesus save me,' Caskie said, his lungs resisting his attempts to breathe, a small choking noise coming from his throat.

The car keys – they were in his pockets! It was a nightmare, he was being punished for all his sins, God was doing this to him, it wasn't fair, oh God please forgive me . . .

He blundered into the bar and found the bottle and took a quick drink, chest leaning on the bar counter, panting heavily. He couldn't go through the man's pockets, he couldn't *touch* him, he would die if he touched him, oh God. He tilted the bottle and let the acrid American whisky run into his throat.

And then he heard a different voice.

'Of course you'll hang five of them to save your own neck,' it said.

'Who's that?' he shouted, turning the torch beam on to the silent tables, flashing the light round the walls. 'They'll call you Judas but you won't worry about that because you'll be breathing and they'll be rotting in their graves. Drink up, McCaskie.'

'My name's Caskie no' McCaskie,' he screamed, throwing the bottle at where the voice had come from and running out of the bar, through the foyer, out into the wind, the voice still behind him, an old man's voice saying evil things in a warm, ingratiating tone. He ran through the rain and wind, stumbling and tripping but always getting up to run again, weightless, as in a dream.

In that eternal moment when death stares you in the face he knew why he was weightless. He was falling. Before he had time to scream he hit the big slabs at the bottom of the deep quarry . . .

A post-mortem revealed that Robert McIver, aged fifty-one, a former captain in the Black Watch, had died of a heart attack brought on by alcoholic poisoning. James

Caskie, aged thirty-one, the well-known Scottish sporting celebrity, had also been drinking heavily before he stumbled over the edge of the quarry in the dark. Death had been instantaneous, almost every bone in his body having been broken by the impact of the stones.

Two weeks later the Horseshoe Inn was gutted in a fire started by teenage vandals.